ALSO BY JAMIL JAN KOCHAI

99 Nights in Logar

The
Haunting
of
Hajji Hotak

and Other Stories

JAMIL JAN KOCHAI

VIKING

VIKING
An imprint of Penguin Random House LLC
penguinrandomhouse.com

The following stories have been previously published, some in slightly different
form: "Playing *Metal Gear Solid V: The Phantom Pain*" in *The New Yorker* (2019);
"Hungry Ricky Daddy" in *Ploughshares* (2018); "Saba's Story" in *The Sewanee
Review* (2019); "A Premonition; Recollected" in *South Asian Avant-Garde* (2020);
"The Haunting of Hajji Hotak" in *The New Yorker* (2021).

Library of Congress Cataloging-in-Publication Data

Names: Kochai, Jamil Jan, 1992– author.
Title: The haunting of Hajji Hotak : and other stories / Jamil Jan Kochai.
Other titles: Haunting of Hajji Hotak (Compilation)
Description: [New York]: Viking, [2022]
Identifiers: LCCN 2022011156 (print) | LCCN 2022011157 (ebook) |
ISBN 9780593297193 (hardcover) | ISBN 9780593297209 (ebook)
Subjects: LCGFT: Short stories.
Classification: LCC PS3611.O343 H38 2022 (print) |
LCC PS3611.O343 (ebook) | DDC 813/.6—dc23/eng/20220307
LC record available at https://lccn.loc.gov/2022011156
LC ebook record available at https://lccn.loc.gov/2022011157

Printed in the United States of America
2nd Printing

DESIGNED BY MEIGHAN CAVANAUGH

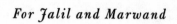

For Jalil and Marwand

So where are you going?

THE HOLY QURAN 81:26

CONTENTS

The Haunting of Hajji Hotak

and Other Stories

Playing *Metal Gear Solid V: The Phantom Pain*

First, you have to gather the cash to preorder the game at the local GameStop where your cousin works, and even though he hooks it up with the employee discount, the game is still a bit out of your price range because you've been using your Taco Bell paychecks to help your pops, who's been out of work since you were ten and who makes you feel unbearably guilty about spending money on useless hobbies while kids in Kabul are destroying their bodies to build compounds for white businessmen and warlords—but, shit, it's Kojima, it's *Metal Gear,* so, after scrimping and saving (like literal dimes you're picking up off the street), you've got the cash, which you give to your cousin, who purchases the game on your behalf, and then, on the day it's released, you just have to find a way to get to the store.

But because your oldest brother has taken the Civic to Sac State, you're hauling your two-hundred-and-sixty-pound ass on a bicycle you haven't touched since middle school, regretting all the Taco Bell you've eaten over the past two years, but, thank Allah (if He's up there), you ride with such fervor that you end up second in line, and it's your cousin himself who hands you the game in a brown paper bag, as if it were something illegal or illicit, which it isn't, of course, it's *Metal Gear,* it's Kojima, it's the final game in a series so fundamentally a part of your childhood that often, when you hear the Irish Gaelic chorus from "The Best Is Yet to Come," you cannot help weeping softly into your keyboard.

For some reason, riding back home is easier.

You leave the bike behind the trash cans at the side of your father's house and hop the wooden fence into the backyard, and if the garage door is locked, which it is, you've got to take a chance on the screen door in the backyard, but, lo and behold, your father is ankle-deep in the dirt, hunched over, yanking at weeds with his bare hands the way he used to as a farmer in Logar, before war and famine forced him to flee to the western coast of the American empire, where he labored for many years until it broke his body for good, and even though his doctor has forbidden him to work in the yard, owing to the torn nerves in his neck and spine—which, you know from your mother, were first damaged when he was tortured by Russians shortly after the murder of his younger brother, Watak, during the Soviet war—he is out here clawing at the earth and its spoils, as if he were digging for treasure or his own grave.

Spotting you only four feet away from the sliding glass door, he gestures for you to come over, and though you are tired and sweaty, with your feet aching and the most important game of the decade hidden inside your underwear, you approach him.

He signals for you to crouch down beside him, then he runs his dirty fingers through his hair until flakes of his scalp fall onto his shoulders and his beard.

This isn't good.

. . .

When your father runs his hands through his hair, it is because he has forgotten his terrible, flaking dandruff, which he forgets only during times of severe emotional or physical distress, which means that he is about to tell you a story that is either upsetting or horrifying or both, which isn't fair, because you are a son and not a therapist.

Your father is a dark, sturdy man and so unlike you that, as a child, you were sure that one day Hagrid would come to your door and inform you of your status as a Mudblood, and then your true life—the life without the weight of your father's history, pain, guilt, hopelessness, helplessness, judgment, and shame—would begin.

Your father asks you where you were.

"The library."

"You have to study?"

You tell him you do, which isn't, technically, a lie.

———

.   .   .

"All right," he says in English, because he has given up on speaking to you in Pashto, "but, after you finish, come back down. I have something I need to talk to you about."

Hurry.

When you get to your room, you lock the door and turn up MF Doom on your portable speaker to ward off mothers, fathers, grandmothers, sisters, and brothers who want to harp at you about prayer, Quran, Pashto, Farsi, a new job, new classes, exercise, basketball, jogging, talking, guests, chores, homework help, bathroom help, family time, and usually *Madvillainy* does the trick.

Open the brown paper bag and toss the kush your cousin has stashed with your game because he needs a new smoking buddy and he sees you as a prime target, probably because he thinks you've got nothing better to do with your time or you're not as religious as your brothers or you're desperate to escape the unrelenting nature of a corporeal existence, and—goddamn, the physical map of Afghanistan that comes with the game is fucking beautiful.

.
.

Not that you're a patriot or a nationalist or one of those Afghans who walk around in a pakol and kameez and play the tabla and claim that their favorite singer is Ahmad Zahir, but the fact that 1980s Afghanistan is the final setting of the most legendary and artistically significant gaming franchise in the history of time made you all the more excited to get your hands on it, especially since you've been shooting at Afghans in *Call of Duty* for so long that you've become oddly immune to the self-loathing you felt when you were first massacring wave after wave of militant fighters who looked just like your father.

Now, finally, start the game.

After escaping the hospital massacre, you and Revolver Ocelot travel to the brutal scenes of northern Kabul—its rocky cliffs, its dirt roads, and its sunlight bleeding off into the dark mountains just the way you remember from all those years ago when you visited as a child—and although your initial mission is to locate and extract Kazuhira Miller, *The Phantom Pain* is the first *Metal Gear* to be set in an open-world environment, and you decide to postpone the rescue of Kazuhira Miller until you get some Soviet blood on your hands.

Your father, you know, didn't kill a single Russian during his years as a mujahid in Logar, but there is something in the act of slaughtering these Soviet NPCs that makes you feel connected to him and his history of warfare.

Thinking of your father and his small village in Logar, you head south to explore the outer limits of the open world in *The Phantom Pain,* crossing trails and deserts and mountain passes, occasionally stopping at a checkpoint or a military barracks to slaughter more Russians, and you find yourself, incredibly, skirting the city of Kabul, still dominated by the Soviets, and continuing on to Logar, to Mohammad Agha, and when you get to Wagh Jan, the roadside-market village that abuts the Kabul–Logar highway, just the way you remember it, you hitch your horse and begin to sneak along the clay compounds and the shops, climbing walls and crawling atop roofs, and whenever a local Afghan spots you, you knock him out with a tranquilizer, until you make it to the bridge that leads to the inner corridors of your parents' home village, Naw'e Kaleh, which looks so much like the photos and your own blurred memories from the trip when you were a kid that you begin to become uneasy, not yet afraid, but as if consumed by an overwhelming sense of déjà vu.

Sneaking along dirt roads, past golden fields and apple orchards and mazes of clay compounds, you come upon the house where your father used to reside, and it is there—on the road in front of your father's home—that you spot Watak, your father's sixteen-year-old brother, whom you recognize only because his picture (unsmiling, head shaved, handsome, and sixteen forever) hangs on the wall of the room in your home where your parents pray.

But here he is, in your game, and you press Pause and you set down the controller, and now you are afraid.

Sweat is running down your legs in rivulets, in streams, your heart is thumping, and you are wondering if sniffing the kush as you did earlier has got you high.

You look out the window and see your brother walking toward the house in the dark, and you realize that you've been playing for too long.

. . .

You're blinking a lot.

Too much.

You notice that your room is a mess and that it smells like ass and that you've become so accustomed to its smell and its mess that from the space inside your head, behind your eyes, the space in which your first-person POV is rooted, you—

Ignore the knock.

It's just your little sister.

Get back to the game.

There is a bearded, heavyset man beside Watak, who, you soon realize, is your father.

You pause the game again and put down the controller.

———

. . .

Doom spits, "His life is like a folklore legend. . . . Why you so stiff, you need to smoke more, bredrin . . . instead of trying to riff with the broke war veteran."

It seems to you a sign.

You extract the kush from the trash, and, because you have no matches or lighter, you put hunks of it in your mouth and you chew and nearly vomit twice.

Return to the game.

Hiding in your grandfather's mulberry tree, you listen to your father and his brother discuss what they will eat for suhoor, thereby indicating that it is still Ramadan, that this is just days before Watak's murder.

Then it hits you.

Here is what you're going to do: before your father is tortured and his brother murdered, you are going to tranquilize them both and you are going to carry them to your horse and cross Logar's terrain until you reach a safe spot where you can call a helicopter and fly them back to your offshore platform: Mother Base.

But just as you load your tranquilizers, your brother bangs on your door and demands that you come out, and after ignoring him for a bit, which only makes him madder and louder, you shout that you are sick, but the voice that comes out of your mouth is not your own, it is the voice of a faraway man imitating your voice, and your brother can tell.

He leaves, and you return to the game.

From the cover of the mulberry tree, you aim your tranquilizer gun but forget that you've got the laser scope activated, and Watak sees the red light flashing on your father's chest and they're off, running and firing back at your tree with rifles they had hidden underneath their patus, and you are struck twice, so you need a few moments to recover your health, and by the time you do, they're gone.

.   .   .

Your brother is back, and this time he has brought along your oldest brother, who is able to shout louder and bang harder than your second-oldest brother, and they're both asking what you're doing and why you won't come out and why you won't grow up and why you insist on worrying your mother and your father, who you know gets those terrible migraines triggered by stress, and now your oldest brother is banging so hard you're afraid the door will come off its hinges, so you lug your dresser in front of it as a barricade and then you go back to your spot in front of the TV, and you sit on the floor and press Play.

At night, under cover of darkness, you sneak toward your father's compound, and you scale the fifteen-foot-high walls of clay and crawl along the rooftops until you get to the highest point in the compound, where your father is on the lookout for incoming jets and firebombs, and you shoot him twice in the back with tranquilizers and, as he is falling, you catch him in your arms, your father, who at this time is around the same age that you are now, and in the dark, on the roof of the compound that he will lose to this

12

war, you hold him, his body still strong and well, his heart unbroken, and you set him down gently on the clay so that the sky does not swallow him.

After climbing down into the courtyard, you go from chamber to chamber, spotting uncles and aunts and cousins you've never met in real life, and you find Watak near the cow shed, sleeping just behind the doorway of a room filled with women, as if to protect them, and after you aim your tranquilizer and send Watak into a deeper sleep, your grandmother, a lifelong insomniac, rises from her toshak and strikes you in the shoulder with a machete and calls for the men in the house, of whom there are many, to awaken and slaughter the Russian assassin who has come to kill us all in our sleep.

The damage from the machete is significant.

Nonetheless, you still have the strength to tranquilize your grandmother, pick up Watak, and climb back onto the roof while all your uncles and cousins and even your grandfather are awakened and armed and begin to fire at your legs as you hustle along, bleeding and weary, to the spot where your father rests.

.   .   .

With your uncle on one shoulder and your father on the other, you leap off the roof into the shadows of an apple orchard.

The men are pouring out onto the roads and the fields, calling upon neighbors and allies, and because the orchard is soon surrounded on all sides, it seems certain that you will be captured, but you are saved by, of all things, a squadron of Spetsnaz, who begin to fire on the villagers, and in the confusion of the shoot-out, as the entire village is lit up by a hundred gunfights, each fight a microcosm of larger battles and wars and global conflicts strung together by the invisible wires of beloved men who will die peacefully in their sleep, you make your way out of the orchard, passing trails and streams and rivers and mulberry trees, until you reach your horse and ride out of Wagh Jan, toward an extraction point in the nearby Black Mountains.

But now, at the door, is your father.

"Mirwais?" he is saying, very gently, the way he used to say it when you were a kid, when you were in Logar, when you got the flu, when the pills and the IV and the home remedies weren't working, when there was nothing to do but wait for the aching to ebb, and your father was there, maybe in the orchard, maybe on the veranda, and he was holding you in his lap, running his fingers through your hair, and saying your name, the way he is saying it now, as if it were almost a question.

"Mirwais?" he says, and, when you do not reply, nothing else.

Keep going.

Russians chase you on the ground and in the air, they fire and you are struck once, twice, three or four times, and there are so many Russians, but your horse is quick and nimble and manages the terrain better than their trucks can, and you make it to the extraction point, in a hollow of the Black Mountains, with enough time to summon the helicopter and to set up a perimeter of mines, and you hide your father and his brother at the mouth of a cave, behind a large boulder the shape of a believer in prostration, where you lie prone with a sniper rifle and begin to pick off Russian paratroopers in the distance, and you fire at the engines of the trucks and ignore the tanks, which will reach you last, and it is mere moments before your helicopter will arrive, and just when you think you are going to make it, your horse is slaughtered in a flurry of gunfire and your pilot is struck by a single bullet from a lone rifleman, and the helicopter falls to the earth and bursts into flames, killing many Russians and giving you just enough time to rush into the cave, into the heart of the Black Mountains.

With your father on one shoulder and your uncle on the other, and with the lights of the Soviet gunfire dying away at the outer edges of your vision, you trudge deeper into the darkness of the cave, and though you cannot be sure that your father and his brother are still alive, that they haven't been shot in the chaos, that they are not, now, corpses, you feel compelled to keep moving into a darkness so complete that your reflection becomes visible on the screen of the television in front of you, and it is as if the figures in the image were journeying inside you, delving into your flesh.

TO BE SAVED. ♦

Return to Sender

Though Dr. Yusuf Ibrahimi hadn't offered a salah since his big bearded father died from a perfectly curable ailment almost a decade ago, he still awoke every Fajr adhan to wage an ongoing war with the ghost of his father's beard. Once shaved and bandaged, Yusuf headed into the kitchen for two cups of tea and some light reading. And it was there, in the kitchen of his apartment in Kabul, that he heard the first knock. The muffled thud—just the one—came so quietly, so unexpectedly, and so early in the morning that Yusuf initially wondered if he misheard the sound altogether. Some sort of a phantom thump belonging to the djinn Yusuf hadn't believed in since his sophomore year at UC Berkeley. For a few moments, he sat in the kitchen, at his table, his thumb pressed firmly upon the corner of the second page of an existential treatise he would give up on forever within the week, and he looked from the table, through the hall, past his son's bedroom, toward the sturdy steel door of his rather large apartment, and he waited. He was waiting, of course, for the second knock, but several moments later, when it did not come, he relented.

Peeping out into the hallway, first left, then right, Yusuf nearly overlooked the small cardboard box lying just a few inches away from his recently swollen pinky toe.

Well, I hope this isn't a bomb, Yusuf thought to himself, and nearly laughed.

●
○

Amina was dreaming.

She worked night shifts at the hospital and slept in the mornings, never having been so tired in her life. Since their move to Kabul six months ago, it seemed as if the entirety of their local hospital had been hoisted upon her and Yusuf alone. Six doctors, eleven nurses, eight midwives, an assisting staff of fifteen, and an absolutely unfathomable number of patients. In the beginning, the young couple had thrown themselves wholly into their labors. Amina worked the nights. Yusuf handled the days. And their lives seemed to orbit around the hospital like two alternate moons. When one came, the other left. When one woke, the other slept. When they spoke it was either about the hospital or their eight-year-old: Ismael. And even, on occasion, when they made love, it seemed to be done out of a grave necessity, like wearied pilgrims sent into the seas for land. If there was any resentment to be had, neither of them expressed or acknowledged it. This was their debt, Amina thought, their yearlong trial.

Amina had been trained as a pediatrician, but over the past six months she had performed amputations, cauterizations, two unauthorized vasectomies, and a secret assisted suicide not even her husband knew about. She had seen patients walk into her hospital, without any assistance, carrying with them the wreckage of their own torn limbs. She burned herself seven times touching melted flesh. She carried men once twice her size but halved in two onto gurneys and beds and sometimes, when there was nothing else, just a thin blanket upon the floor. She heard soldiers and militants sob like children and had seen little dark boys look upon their lost hands or feet with a wonder that seemed almost holy in the time of its happening. In fact, so many children had died under her care, or in her very hands—their eyes, their eyelashes, staring up into her life, on the edge of death, and then no longer the edge, but in the heart of the Thing itself—that they had begun to alter the way she looked upon her only son, Ismael, whose features, she had to admit, had become more and more muddled with the passing months. Some mornings, after a particularly brutal shift, Amina would sneak into Ismael's room and linger by his bed. Then, with her eyes closed, she would search under his sheets for his fingers or his feet, and when she found them, she would almost sob for their softness.

Having awoken from a pleasant dream, Amina did not rise when she first heard a series of muffled knocks come from the sturdy door of her rather large apartment. The bedroom ceiling fan above her held still in the sweltering heat. As usual, the electricity in her building had gone out sometime before Fajr. She lived in a relatively well-guarded apartment complex just off Kart-e Naw road, atop a hill almost as steep as her rent, which, her landlord claimed, paid for the security, the amenities (indoor plumbing and a gas stove), the currently out-of-order elevator, and the quality of the neighborhood: mostly civil servants, business professionals, and other members of the Kabuli upper-lower middle class. To Amina's joy, there was hardly a foreigner among them.

Still slightly intoxicated by the logic of her dreams, for several moments Amina attempted to move the blades of her ceiling fan telepathically. The muffled knocking persisted. She sat up, her feet hanging over the edge of her bed. Out of her six sisters, Amina was both the darkest and the shortest, and from a young age, she understood that there was no helping this. Rather than wallow in her seeming misfortune, she never avoided sunlight, never missed a class, never gave any boys any time (save, eventually, for Yusuf), and she stretched every single morning to maintain her soldier's posture.

It was because of these stretches that Amina, at first, did not answer the door. Then it was because she thought her husband would. Then, guessing that Yusuf had left a few minutes early for the hospital, Amina realized she had not gone to the door simply because she was afraid. Ashamed of this fear, she tossed on a white chador (the type her mother used to wear) and went to welcome her visitor.

In the hall, atop a fading mat left behind by a previous tenant, she immediately spotted what she did not know was the second package delivered to her door that morning.

"Yusuf," she called back into her apartment, just to be sure. Hearing no reply, she picked up the small cardboard box and carried it into the kitchen, placing it carefully on the table right beside her husband's open copy of *The Myth of Sisyphus,* which he read in spite of the fact that Amina had explained to him that Camus was a racist.

"And Aristotle was a child rapist," Yusuf had countered, though Amina was not sure how that belied her point.

The package had no address or name. She did not know if it was meant for her or her husband, and she was not the type to pry.

But as Amina turned to leave the kitchen to check on Ismael, she happened to glance, very quickly, in the direction of the cardboard box nestled between the Camus and the chai, which at that exact moment almost seemed to shudder. The movement was so slight that Amina immediately doubted whether she actually saw it. The box became still again. But by that point she could not help herself. She approached the package as if it were a small, wounded bird, then, lifting it in her left hand, she tore the clear tape bound to its lid and found inside the box, wrapped in butcher paper, without note or name or reason, the severed index finger of her only child, whose name, to her horror, she suddenly forgot.

Ismael.

His name was Ismael.

Staring down at Ismael's severed finger, still etched with henna, Amina could not know that this was the second finger delivered to her door that morning.

.
.

The first finger was with her husband, Yusuf, who, sixteen stories beneath her, was hobbling down the last four flights of the apartment building stairway. In a rush to capture the deliverer of the package, he had tripped and injured his ankle at the beginning of the first flight. Their elevator had been out of order since the bombing two weeks ago. If they lived in one of the fortified bases he had recommended— with the other Americans, the private military and corporate contractors, the journalists, diplomats, expatriates, and all the other fortunate professionals who had the sense to understand that they were living in a war zone and not a tourist destination—there would have been nothing to worry about. But Amina had to be among *her* people. Even if it meant risking their lives. And so Yusuf found himself hobbling down the last flight of stairs on what he almost certainly knew was a fractured ankle. Despite the pulsing of the pain in his leg, he nearly sprinted out of his building, into the parking lot of his complex, where his neighbors were all abustle with a hundred different tasks, one of which, he knew, was related to the delivery of the package he carried in his hands.

Thanks to the Eid al-Adha holiday, there were also children in the lot. Hundreds of them. They had turned the parking lot of the complex into a makeshift cricket tournament. There were probably twenty games going on at once. The children ran their matches between cars and shops, in the alleys between buildings, in the center of walkways, always, it seemed, on the brink of scattering. From the outset, Yusuf had found these children irritating. Their cursing, spitting, slapping, screaming, always screaming, and their staring, like they knew he didn't belong. Their proclivity for violence and disease. Their whole unsupervised existence. But now, with his son missing, the boy's finger wrapped in a delicate piece of butcher paper, Yusuf despised these children with a rage he was afraid he could not control. Fortunately, the nearest guard's post was in the opposite direction of the games. There, a dark and stout policeman watched rivers of civilians pour into and out of the gates, unbeknownst to the fact that he had almost certainly allowed a butcherer to pass through his gate. Yusuf rushed this policeman and shouted, in his broken Farsi, that his child was missing.

The policeman replied in Pashto.

"My boy is *missing*," Yusuf repeated in Farsi.

The policeman said something else in Pashto, laughed, and then pointed toward the cricket tournaments.

"No," Yusuf shouted in English, "he's been kidnapped."

The policeman seemed more bewildered than before.

Finally, Yusuf thought to show him the finger.

●
●

Amina was still in the kitchen, balancing Ismael's second finger in the center of her palm. The entire digit had been cut precisely at its base, as if in a surgical operation. The finger did not bleed. But it was not the lack of blood, nor the precision of the cut, nor the odd fluorescence of the butcher paper, nor the arrival of the package itself that had paralyzed Amina.

No.

Amina could not move because the severed finger in the palm of her hand seemed to be slowly curling into and out of itself. What a wonder (Amina felt but could not think) that she was even able to stand, to breathe, and that her ligaments and her bones and the muscles holding together these ligaments and these bones did not collapse into themselves. The finger curled. She knew it was curling because the butcher paper crinkled with its movements. She saw the curling of the finger with the eyes in the sockets of her skull, and she heard the crinkling of the butcher paper with the ears on the sides of her head, still covered, she realized, with the white chador.

That was when she heard the second knock.

She rushed to the door, where, out in the hall, atop her mat, she found another small cardboard box. This time, it was an ear. As with the finger, its cut was precise, surgical, and though at first it did not move, when Amina took up the ear in its butcher paper and brought it close to her lips and whispered, "Where is the rest of you?" the ear in her palm seemed to pulse.

Yusuf did not understand the question.

"What do you want me to do with this?" the police commander asked, again, in Farsi, gesturing to the cardboard box sitting on his desk.

Yusuf's ankle was swelling. He should not have been

able to walk on it at all, but he'd still managed to hobble from the gate of his apartment complex, down the road, slipping into an open sewer and further aggravating his ankle, toward the taxis, one of which kindly gave him a ride to the block just outside the police station. He made his way through seven security checkpoints, and at each checkpoint he was almost shot while attempting to explain the situation with the box and the finger in his broken Farsi. Not a single policeman could tell him what to do, and instead each policeman kept directing him to meet with another policeman of a higher ranking until, finally, he reached the office of the head policeman, who, for the third time, and only out of respect for the doctor's background, patiently repeated his question:

"What do you want me to do with this?"

"It's my son's finger," he said. "It's in a box."

Yusuf sat in a steel chair, barefoot, stinking of sewage and sweat, his pant legs stained, his shirt collar torn open by repeated manhandlings, his cheeks bruised, his forehead bloodied, and his beard, somehow, already returned.

"I know," the police commander said. "I read the report. But, Doctor Sahib, you have to understand. Usually with these cases there's a note. A demand. A number to call. Usually the kidnapper or kidnappers provide instructions, and we work with those, and it makes the whole ordeal manageable. But there are no demands here. So, I'm not sure what you want us to do."

"An alarm," Yusuf said, trying to think of the proper Farsi term. "I have pictures. There should be a search. An announcement."

The police commander's mustache seemed to twitch. His thin hair was slicked back, which made his enormous forehead appear even larger.

"Listen," Yusuf said, raising his voice. "I'm an American citizen. My son is an American citizen. This should not just be considered a kidnapping. This is an act of terrorism. Isn't that your job? Aren't you paid to capture terrorists? Why are you sitting here, in your office, asking me what I want you to do? Do what you do. Or. Or. I'll take this to the embassy. To the consulate. I swear to God I'll have you fired."

"Where do you think you are?" the police commander asked, very calm. "My American friend, do you know how many people have walked into this station, this very day, to report their missing children? Do you understand that if we did a search for every missing child reported to us, that the search would never end, that all the workings of this country would stop as they were, and that there would be no one left to protect the city from insurgents? No. Listen. Do you understand that if every single policeman in this city was to search day and night, search every apartment room, every alley, that the missing children would still never be found? You must trust me, Doctor Sahib, there is no demand because there is no purpose, because your kidnappers are fucking with you. Whether you report me to your embassy or not, your son is gone. Hopefully dead. You should be home now, praying."

The police commander took a deep and solemn breath, as if he were not used to speaking for such an extended length of time.

"I don't pray," Yusuf said, almost to himself.

"Well," the police commander replied, his face for the first time overcome with pity, "there's nothing else I can do for you. Go home and wait for further instruction."

Out on the street, Yusuf stood near the corner of an intersection as several taxi drivers, some Pashtun, some Farsiwan, halted next to him, asked if he needed a ride, and then sped away with a muttered curse when Yusuf replied, incomprehensibly, in English.

"These foreigners," they all said in one way or another.

Across the street, in the center of the second road, lay circular markings of black ash. Remnants, Yusuf thought, from the suicide bombing that had occurred in this area just a few weeks ago. It had been a small operation. The bomber, intending to rush the police compound, was immediately spotted by a sniper and shot in his shoulder, but before he fell, he managed to flip his trigger. A few bystanders were injured, bloodied, but only the bomber himself was killed. Thinking of this man, imagining what horrors had led him to that spot in the street with that fire tied to his belly, Yusuf walked out onto the intersection, toward the black markings. When he reached the center of the circular ash, fading, yes, but also embedded, Yusuf cupped the small cardboard box in his hands, near his gut, and he sat with his legs folded in the middle of the street. Two poor taximen, thinking Yusuf a beggar, dropped coins in his lap.

.
.

Only six miles away, Amina sat on Ismael's bed, near his open window, tinted red for no reason at all, and she waited for time to pass into sound. Outside, twenty stories below her, hundreds of young boys, and even a few girls, some of them wealthy, some of them hungry and ill, screamed and laughed with such a relentless fervor that it seemed as if their very lives depended upon the intensity of their joy. Amina had been waiting all morning as, one after the other, the muffled knocks sounded from the door, and each time she rushed to answer it, again, at the bottom of the doorway, atop her mat, she found another package, inside of which was another pulsing piece of Ismael's still living body. She had collected these pieces together, and on the bed where Ismael once slept and dreamed and sometimes played, she reorganized the body of her child, piece by piece by piece.

In the beginning, she had seemed almost dazed by her labors, hypnotized, but in reality, she floated throughout the doorways of her apartment, her white chador fluttering about her legs, in a state of utter focus. She found that every twenty-third thump of her heart aligned perfectly with the sound of the knocks from the door. Soon, she came to feel that her hands and her feet, her lungs and her blood, were not at all working in unison, directed by the will of her singular mind, but that each limb was willingly acting on its own. And she felt so very gracious that the threads of her hair did not leap off her head and that her fingernails did not fall away from their beds and that her heart, pumping and pumping, day and night, was not forlorn, was not driven to suicide by the traumas and monotonies of her short, short life. She recalled a story, unsure if it was from the Quran or Sahih al-Bukhari, of how, on Judgment Day, your hand and your mouth and your eyes were supposed to testify against you, proclaiming your sins before the judgment of Allah. What a story, she used to think. But now she felt she was becoming untethered from her body, and for moments at a time, she played with the idea that she was not awake at all. That this, too, was a long dream, but then she would open another package and watch the curling, wriggling, pulsing of the flesh, and her faith in the reality of the moment would be reaffirmed.

How odd, she thought, that she ever doubted.

In between each knock, Amina had a few moments at a time to examine the possessions in Ismael's room. The journals of daily contemplation (Yusuf). The *Shahnameh* (Amina). His water paintings of the Kabul River (Amina). His baseball mitt (Yusuf) and his cricket bat (Amina). His puzzles (Yusuf) and his collection of poetry (Amina). She scoured through these projects and books and obligatory hobbies, until she found (hidden inside of a mutilated Farsi–English dictionary) a handheld game console. After turning it on, she saw that the dual-screened device contained videos. Clips of Ismael roaming the complex, of children playing cricket in the parking lot, of shop owners and taximen who knew Ismael by name. These were shot in the daylight. But there were also grainy videos of him crawling out his window in the night and then climbing down a ledge into the empty apartment below him. From there, Ismael snuck out into the hall and made his way toward the parking lot. The clips she watched were short. No more than a minute at a time. She witnessed Ismael roaming the streets of Kabul, meeting with older boys, speaking Farsi fluently, stealing chips and ice cream from vendors, throwing stones at stray dogs and soldiers, cursing drivers, pissing in the sewers, visiting graveyards in the hills, chasing after armored Humvees, sneaking onto buses, traveling from one route to the next until he made it all the way to the hospital where his parents worked, and there he recorded Amina's labor. In one of the last videos, Amina watched herself, sitting outside a patient's room, sobbing into her hands because she had just helped the gut-shot fourteen-year-old gunman kill himself so that he wouldn't be tortured by the NDS in his final minutes. Ismael must only have been a few yards away from her.

She had never seen him.

By noon, Amina had managed to collect a hundred and thirty-seven boxes, and the contents of these boxes were spread out on Ismael's bed. Fingers and toes and a tuft of his hair. Teeth. A few of them at a time. His nose. His lips. His tongue. Quartered sections of his abdomen. There didn't seem to be any order to it. Once, she received half of a palm. Then a single toe. And in one package she received three eyelashes. Gradually, with the shreds of Ismael she had collected from the packages, Amina was able to piece together entire sections of his body. An arm. A leg. His feet. These sections she stitched together using the surgical suture she kept in her bedroom, and, oddly enough, she found that when she stitched two bits of Ismael together, they stopped pulsing. Knock by knock by knock, a thud at a time, she stitched together his torso and his arms and his legs and his neck and his face and his scalp and his lips and his nose and almost every single part of him save for a single finger she was sure would arrive toward the end of the knocking.

But then the end came and there was still a finger missing. The rhythm of the knocks faded and every twenty-third thump of her heart ached her savagely. Noon became Dhuhr as the adhan for the jummah prayer rang out from their complex's mosque. Local believers and, she was sure, nonbelievers, too, rushed into the mosque, huddled in their prayers, and fled back home. She waited for the knock and listened to the surahs of the salah, whose meaning she had never learned. Her limbs began to weigh on her. She sat and watched the remnants of Ismael's still living body on the bed. Over the minaret's speakerphone, the imam bade salaam to the angels, and after the prayer was finally finished, there was such a billowing silence in the complex, in her apartment, inside her chest, that it drove Amina to locate her husband's straight razor, and so, upon returning to her child's side, she unsheathed the blade, lifted her index finger, and felt the need to explain.

The plan was to spend one year.

One year, she had told Yusuf, to repay their debts to the land from which they had fled. The land left to calamity. But even in college, she had suspected that Yusuf's activism was partly an act. He was tall and pretty, and his heroic rhetoric always felt like a sort of bravado, as if he said what he did merely to befriend her. They rallied against the Taliban. They penned strongly worded letters to Mullah Omar. They lent each other notes for exams, papers, and eventually poetry. They drank chai and read Rumi. But with time, as their education became more intense and focused, the rallies fell away, and Yusuf's activist spirit seemed to die. Whenever Amina mentioned helping Kabul, Yusuf came up with one excuse after another. First applications, then interviews, then med school, then the wedding, the honeymoon, Italy, France, Ismael's birth, Ismael's schooling, the second pregnancy, the miscarriage, and after that, for a while, she secretly appreciated the excuses, how they eased the weight of her conscience. Until one night when she read an Al Jazeera article about the Afghan government's gradual loss of land to the Taliban. The US military had been skewing statistics in order to make it seem as if Kabul still had a strong hold on most of the country, but apparently the Taliban controlled or contested territory in more than seventy percent of provinces. The jihadists seemed to be winning the war. She worried that one day the Taliban might very well take Kabul itself, and she felt a terrible urgency to repay her debts to the homeland before her country was lost, again, to the fanatics. Without telling Yusuf, she booked the tickets. One year. She promised him. Just the one. But now, it seemed to Amina (as she knelt near Ismael's bed, her husband's razor digging into her index finger) that their time in Kabul was to be cut precisely in half. That was when she heard the last knock.

Amina—unlike Ismael—bled profusely.

Still, she rushed to the door.

Standing ragged in the hallway, bloodied and broken, was Yusuf, and in his hand was the final package. Quietly,

Amina took Yusuf's arm and led him to the bedroom where Ismael lay, no longer pulsing, and she tore open the last box and carefully lifted Ismael's finger, which trembled inconsolably in her palm, and while Yusuf sat on the other side of Ismael, holding his son's wrist as if he meant to feel for his pulse, Amina took up her thread and needle as Ismael's entire body, every single sutured piece of him, began to shiver so violently that Amina could not steady the hand upon which she needed to stitch the first and final finger, and so, seeing his place in the scheme, Yusuf came to Amina's side and held with her the trembling hand. Together, piercing and threading, tearing and binding, flesh to flesh, Amina and Yusuf both realized that they would never leave Kabul again, that they were home.

Enough!

Rangeena does not know what to say to her brute of a son who will not stop shouting about pills or land or a stolen envelope of cash he meant to donate to the orphans of Logar because he's rambling now absolutely rambling in front of her beloved daughters come all the way from Fremont to visit Rangeena in this lonesome living room her son has decided to paint the most despicable shade of blue, just sitting there, the poor girls, watching their old mother get harangued by her only living son on the earth, who is shouting: "I found the torn envelope in your drawer of photos . . . ," and of course there's no way for her to respond to all of his accusations without weeping like the child she had been, once married off to a sixty-year-old nomad at the precious age of fifteen or fourteen or who knows how old, exactly, though Rangeena did recall she was not too old to be playing with the dolls she fashioned out of clay from the edges of the rivers near where her youngest son would one day be murdered, when her mother approached her in a coat of ash or dust or snowflakes and informed her that within the year she would be married and moved and pregnant, again and again, pregnant, leading to so many little unmarked graves in the apple orchard, beneath the falling blossoms, as if Allah (all

Praise

Be

To

Him) were saying look I know I know but then there's this, until the babies stopped dying with the birth of her eldest son, the survivor, the rambler, still somehow rambling beneath the half-lit ceiling light he has failed to fix for the past three months no matter how many times Rangeena moans, "This darkness will swallow me!" his massive frame blocking the television and the fake fireplace and the cabinet containing Rangeena's favorite photograph of Watak, his head shaved, his mustache barely sprouted, his soft lashes sparkling with frost, his lips slightly parted as if he is about to speak, but then his older brother, the survivor, speaks in his place, rambling about the pink pills from the Target CVS instead of the pharmacy at Raley's, which was where Dr. Ahmadzi had sent all her medications before he died, before her eldest son moved the family out of their three-bedroom house in Broderick to their five-bedroom house in Bridgeway, despite the fact that she secretly preferred the smaller house and the bigger bedroom she shared with her eldest grandson, just six at the time, and so meek and so gentle he would hold her hand every night to fall asleep, and then there were the ancient oak trees in the backyard and Faisal market down the road, only a mile or so, a fifteen-minute walk for some dried mulberries or kishmish or fresh bread or a conversation with another Afghan, while in Bridgeway she was surrounded for miles by nothing but houses, her white neighbors and their houses, her white neighbors and their dogs and their houses, their vicious dogs, always barking, always yapping and lunging, always on the brink of tearing away from their owners to rip open her insides like she had seen the Communists' dogs do in the pits of the orchards where her children had picked apples while searching for her eldest son who, thank Allah (all

———

Praise

Be

To

Him), was not eaten by those dogs or blown to pieces by the bombs or shot near the bank of a stream, her white neighbors' dogs preventing her from going outside and taking a walk and shedding the pounds piled up on her belly and back and thighs and, she supposes, the valves of her heart, otherwise why wouldn't her son stop rambling that she had forgotten to take her blood pressure meds or had accidentally hidden them in the sheets of her bed, only for her son's snoop of a wife to find them one day and claim that Rangeena was hoarding them to gift to her only living sibling on the earth, who, yes, perhaps, is an addict and a swindler and a wifebeater, but who also has very severe heart problems, and when you consider the state of Logar, that is, the ongoing years of bombings and shootings and random roadside executions, the Khalqian, the Soviets, the mujahideen, the Taliban, and the Americans, well, how could you blame her poor brother for deciding to steal (is it even stealing?) a small slice of the land that should rightfully belong as much to her as it does to her son, the rambler, and his viper of a wife, always watching, always listening, whispering, informing Rangeena's brute of a son whether or not Rangeena is taking her pills or stockpiling her napkins or shutting off her oxygen tank to keep it from overheating or waking up in the night unable to breathe or telling the truth on the phone to her daughters or spitting loogies directly beneath the corners of the carpets where no one looks, except, apparently, for her son's snoop of a wife, a Farsiwan, you know—like Rangeena's mother—a weak-willed woman, her son's wife, laughs at everything, eats your insults, doesn't say shit to your face but then reports every word back to her husband, who rushes Rangeena, big man, rambling about respect and kindness, though he certainly doesn't ramble very respectfully, even now, even in this lonesome living room finally filled up with all her children, rambling in front of her beloved daughters come all the way from Fremont with their little babies just to see her, rambling so loud she can barely hear Alex Trebek say, "On October seventh, 2001, Operation Enduring Freedom began in this country; by December, the US had dropped twelve thousand bombs and missiles," with the weary resignation of a dying man, the same resignation she had seen in the long-haired boys she hid in her home, in the soft grass of the cows' pen, between ambushes and firefights, boys so young they could have been her sons, boys so beautiful they could have been dreams, all of them armed and dying and pretending to be prepared to die, and her son, among them, her eldest son, just as beautiful, just as young, just as resigned to die in the wake of his younger brother's death, but now alive, now old, now ugly, now angry, now pacing up and down the living room, now yanking at his beard, now re-rambling along with her daughters (the traitors!) about the pink pills Rangeena has inadvertently lost, the pills he says are for her heart, but which, in fact, Rangeena found out were for her mind, picking up on the words "anxiety" and "mania" and "panic," words she remembered and repeated to her daughters, her trusting daughters, from whom she learned that the words referred to ailments of the mind, not the body, as if Rangeena had become a madwoman, as if she couldn't beat her entire family at checkers, as if she weren't still memorizing surahs every night and day, as if she weren't at the very peak of her mental faculties, no matter what her son's wife had to say behind her back when she was talking on the phone in the yard, beneath the cherry tree, all day in the yard or in her bedroom or at her brother's house, leaving Rangeena, most days, all on her own, in this house so empty, so dark, so quiet, her grandchildren in their bedrooms, playing games, watching TikTok, leaving her alone with her couch and her breathing tubes and her television and her favorite photo of Watak and her oxygen tank, which, she had heard, can sometimes randomly explode in this house made of sticks, with its fence barely six feet high, barely an inch thick, completely incapable of protecting her from the neighbor's dogs or the registered sex offenders that lived two blocks away, let alone burglars and rapists and Richard Ramírez and Eddie Gallagher and Robert Bales, nothing like the walls of her home in Logar, twenty feet high, four feet thick, and strong enough to withstand rockets and missiles and bullets from the Communists coming for her second-eldest son, Watak, whom, nonetheless, they kill, whom they killed, by the bank of a stream, near the water, rushing water, so heavy, so light, so early in the morning that frost still nipped the leaves, and snow-flakes fell mysteriously from the heavens, as Allah (all

Praise

Be

To

Him) had intended, had always intended, but then there she is, her son's wife, complaining in whispers to her traitorous daughters about having to constantly lift Rangeena's oxygen tank onto her dresser then back onto the floor then back onto her dresser then back onto the floor, about the "aching" in her wrist, as if Rangeena's withered lungs hadn't been ceaselessly aching since the night her body absorbed so much smoke and debris from Soviet cluster bombs she had ash leaking out of her nose and ears and lips, a trail of ash following her from one end of the world to the other, from Logar to Peshawar to Birmingham to Hayward to Broderick to Bridgeway to her favorite seat just in front of the television blocked by her rambling daughters and her rambling son and now *his* rambling son, that is, the very same grandson she had sung to sleep for five years, the same grandson whose ass she had wiped until he was in first grade, until they moved him into a room with his brothers in this too big house, with its too many doors, too many windows, too many lights, too many televisions, too many memories, as in, for example, the night her son's wife discovered that her brothers had been murdered in Logar for nothing, for no one, in snowfall, just a mile or so away from the spot where Watak had been murdered for nothing, for no one, in snowfall, forty years earlier, and Rangeena held her son's wife in her lap and wanted very dearly to tell her the story of how her own younger brother, the jokester, the prankster, laughing at everything, inventing jokes out of dust, out of horror, out of sorrow, had been pinned one snowy day between two trucks in Kabul, how his internal organs had been crushed and bled but his heart kept pumping just long enough for him to look about, to raise his arms, to gesture for help and to whisper a final message into the icy ear of a stranger who disappears forever, who might be dead, who might be living, just waking and sleeping and praying and eating and dying with Rangeena's beloved brother's final words knocking about in his head with a summary of last week's episode of *Ertugrul,* just another memory, a story that begins "But once in Kabul, amid snowflakes, a dying boy gestured . . . ," not knowing that the dying boy was Rangeena's dying brother, that those words, that story, belonged to her, but of course she didn't remind her son's sobbing wife of the story of the death of her brother, or the death of Watak, because Rangeena knew what nobody knew (the weight of his body heavy with water), because she had heard the gunshots from her home, because she had known it was him before she had known it was *him,* because she had rushed onto the wartime roads like a madwoman, her hair unveiled, her nostrils burning with the stink of gunpowder and blood, because—though Watak was twice her size—she had lifted him out of the stream, all sodden and punctured, as light as the day she had birthed him, because Allah (all

Praise

Be

To

Him) grants power to His bereaved, because she was the first to find Watak, as if he were waiting for her, then, now, there, here, her boy, her boys, forever silent, forever rambling, and Rangeena wonders how much longer she is supposed to just sit and suffer her entire family rising up against her before she says *enough,* before she shouts at her rambling son and his whispering wife and her nodding daughters and her muttering grandson *enough,* enough rambling, enough advice, enough pills, enough nightmares, enough lung damage, enough ghosts, enough beautiful dying boys, enough bomb smoke, enough burning apple trees, enough staring white neighbors, enough heavy breathing, enough Watak, enough panic attacks, enough addict brother calling for money, enough spite, enough grudges, enough heartaches, enough dead, enough sins, enough son's wife having to wash her in the tub because she can no longer stand up under her own weight, enough weight, enough waffles, enough Watak, enough ongoing occupation, enough Taliban, enough Bushes, enough Clintons, enough Massouds, enough puppet presidents serving white masters, enough

Watak, enough unanswered prayers, enough brother's jokes turned into sad stories, enough aching in knees, in back, in lungs, in heart, enough breathing tubes, enough inhalers, enough pills, enough beaten mothers, enough gunshots in films, enough wounded, enough babies dying, enough hateful eldest son, enough rambling, enough advising, enough calming, enough loving, enough hating, enough generations of grown children rambling.

"Enough!" Rangeena shouts, and rises up out of her seat and strips off her breathing tubes and limps outside, her children at her back, at her sides, circling and pleading and still somehow rambling, "Where?" over and over, "Where?" Her stupid children and her stupid grandchildren. Her whole stupid family. Too big, too small, too loud, too quiet, too fast, too slow. "To Logar!" she says without saying, and climbs into one of her son's salvaged Civic sedans and grabs the key out of the cup holder where he always keeps it and almost runs over her daughter backing out of the driveway. She straightens the car in the cul-de-sac and spots her son running toward her from the house. Shifting the car into drive, she plans to head down Brother Island Road onto Golden Gate onto Jefferson onto the freeway onto I-80 onto SFO into the international terminal toward the Turkish Airlines ticket counter, where she'll unstitch a seam in her purse and pull out a stolen bundle of cash meant for the orphans of Logar and buy a first-class ticket to Afghanistan. In Kabul, she'll exchange her dollars for afghanis and call for a taxi and pay extra to travel down to Mohammad Agha, to her old village in Naw'e Kaleh, to the bank of the stream where Watak once died, and she'll climb past the chinar trees and down into the water, and stare up at the leaves and the birds and the clouds and the jets and the ghosts and the drones and the angels and the cosmos and Allah (all

Praise

Be

To

Him), and she will float in peace and in silence—except, apparently, for the blasting of a car horn her eldest son had failed to repair only days earlier. The same eldest son is now slumped beside Rangeena in the salvaged Civic she has just crashed into the pole of the lamplight she watches every night from her bedroom. The horn blares louder as the rest of her family surround her car and are once again . . . but her boy . . . her firstborn . . . the one who lived . . . through the cold . . . through the hunger . . . through the mountains . . . through the war . . . her survivor . . . her rambler . . . is so quiet, it stirs her dying body into action. Shards of windshield tumble from her arms and shoulders like the first snowflakes of a new season, as she reaches out to feel for the pulse of her only living son on the earth.

Bakhtawara and Miriam

Upon discovering that her elder sister, the beautiful and clever Zarghoona, who forever afterward would be referred to only as "the Shameless One," had abandoned her American fiancé three days before their wedding, young Bakhtawara of Kabul, overwhelmed by the enormity of Fate, realized that Allah was giving her the blessed opportunity to restore her family's honor by martyring her lovesick heart. Her mother, Gul Sanga, had barely begun sobbing and cursing the next ten generations of Zarghoona's offspring when Bakhtawara came to her side, kissed her tears, and told her that she, Bakhtawara Farhad Niazi, would marry the lonesome boy from America.

But Bakhtawara's mother did not share her daughter's confidence. There were lines of authority to be addressed, which was why Farhad Mohammad Niazi found out that his eldest daughter had run off with Ali the baker just as he learned that his second-eldest daughter, the perpetually somber one, the one whose hair he hadn't seen in two years, had already agreed to save his family's good name. His wife and daughter had sat side by side in front of the television, blocking his favorite Turkish drama, and while Bakhtawara gave him the bad news, Gul Sanga provided the good. In that moment of double discovery, Farhad's heart had almost killed itself before his brain relayed the news that all was not lost, and that even when Allah closed a door, He could tear open a roof.

"Subhanallah," he said, tears cresting his eyes, and without rising from his toshak or looking away from the television, Farhad kissed his daughter's cheek and gave her his blessing.

Final authority, however, still rested with Bakhtawara's eldest brother, Rahman, who had become the unofficial head of the household after taking on a brutalizing job at the local brickyard. Quick-tempered, constantly aching, and slowly being eaten alive by the dust of the bricks with which he fed his father's family, Rahman—not Farhad—had denied Zarghoona's baker and arranged the marriage to Atal. In this way, Rahman planned, his family would be able to outlast the economic drought of the war, and his sister would raise her children in the prosperity of America.

He was set to return from the brickyard within a few hours.

In the meantime, Bakhtawara changed from the hijab she wore around the house to the longer chador she wore for prayers, knotting and layering and swaddling her hair, nearly one meter long, before offering salah in the hall adjacent to the living room, where her younger sister, Shireen, watched Turkish soap operas. Shireen (only occasionally faithful) found her sister's unrelenting piety irksome and would purposefully gossip while she prayed.

"Bakhtawara," Shireen shouted from one room to the next, "I hear that the militias in Mohammad Agha are slaughtered. Nabi is among the victors."

Briefly, Bakhtawara lost track of which surah she was reciting and fell away into a vision of summer days in Logar: picking berries, tossing apples, roasting corn, and singing stories with Nabi, her slender cousin from the countryside. Two years earlier, Nabi had joined a local contingent of the Taliban in Logar to avenge the murder of his older brother, thereby forever squashing Bakhtawara's dreams of marrying him. Rahman was vehemently pro-government and would never allow it. Acting as if she had not heard Shireen, Bakhtawara slipped past her sister and went to visit her neighbor: Miriam.

●
○

Speaking into a small hole in the center of their shared wall, Bakhtawara sat on a mound of flour bags and told Miriam about her plan to wed the boy from America.

"What are the chances," Miriam whispered from her side of the tunnel, "that the boy and his mother agree?"

"Really, it's up to the mother," Bakhtawara replied. "The boy is beholden to her."

"She seems like a cruel woman. I did not want her for Zarghoona, and I want her even less for you."

"I thought she was perfect for Zarghoona. They would laugh for hours."

"A ruse," Miriam said.

"A good one too. I thought she was coming around to the idea of studying in America. It seemed to suit her."

"I told you she was romantic to a fault. Now look at her.

Sacrificed America for a baker. They'll write stories about her someday."

"*Zarghoona and the Baker.*"

"*Bakhtawara and . . .*"

"Atal. His name is Atal," Bakhtawara said.

"I'm sorry, it's just—"

"It's okay. I only memorized his name two days ago. Up until then I wasn't sure if it was Atal or Ajmal, so I just kept referring to him as 'brother.' I was too ashamed to ask anyone for the name of my brother-in-law, and now he'll be my husband."

"How can you be so certain?" Miriam asked.

"This morning, when my mother discovered that Zarghoona had fled, I was still in the middle of my prayer. I had just recited the verse 'And of everything we created pairs, that perhaps you may remember,' and at that moment, upon hearing the news, it was as if I *had* remembered. Not that I had come to some new realization, but truly, Miriam, it was as if a long-forgotten memory had suddenly returned to me. I was to marry Atal. I remembered."

"Nothing is so certain," Miriam replied. "Only Allah knows."

Bakhtawara couldn't fault her neighbor's doubt. Years ago, Miriam had been married to a beautiful but demented civil servant, a friend of her family. Prone to jealousy and paranoia, Miriam's husband demanded that she never leave home without his approval, which he rarely gave. One night, when he discovered that Miriam was sneaking out to visit her cousins, some of whom were once her suitors, he came home early from his shift at the embassy and, after proclaiming his love to her one last time, threw a canister of acid at Miriam's face. The only reason she had not been blinded was that a beam of light from her neighbor's flood lamp had struck her in the eyes just as her husband flung his acid. Her left forearm, seared and bubbling, protected her vision, but her mouth was so severely burned, she could barely scream for help. Her husband fled the compound, the neighborhood, the city, and was never seen again. Miriam's in-laws, perhaps fearing a violent reprisal from her brothers, paid out of pocket for a skin-grafting operation in Peshawar. The surgery was largely successful, restoring her ability to speak and eat, but the scars remained. She returned to her father's home in Kabul, without any restrictions upon her freedom, but by then she had lost all desire to go out. Imprisoning herself within the walls of her compound, Miriam happened one day to come upon a hole in the wall of her bedroom, through which she glanced upon Bakhtawara, who, shamefully curious about the tragic character living beside her, had been spying on Miriam. A blessed mouse must have scampered atop a stack of flour bags and carved the hole in the center of the wall just to tempt the girls with its presence. They had a quick fight, both girls accusing each other of treachery and each promising to cover her side of the hole. But they returned, trading insults and barbs, then jokes and stories, and eventually dreams and memories. From time to time, Bakhtawara would catch a glimpse of Miriam's figure— her legs, her hair, a shadow, a scar—so as to gradually form an incomplete image of her neighbor, and though Bakhtawara had never actually seen Miriam all at once, she knew her voice so well that sometimes, at night, she would awaken to the gentle murmuring of Miriam's sleep talk, and if Miriam went on murmuring for more than a few moments, Bakhtawara would shuffle out of bed, tiptoe to the storage room, and, with her ear gently pressed to the hole in the center of their shared wall, she would listen. Not to spy. But just to be sure that Miriam's dreams were not too sad or fearful, and if they were, she would wake her friend with a story and go on chatting until the morning light.

"Would you attend the wedding?" Bakhtawara asked.

"Only if you hold it in our courtyard," Miriam joked. But when she did not hear Bakhtawara laugh, she went on to whisper: "Inshallah."

•

On the pretext of finding a borrowed bracelet, Bakhtawara carefully searched her sister's room for some clue as to where she might have gone. Originally, it had been Rahman's idea to give Zarghoona her own space and cell phone. A token of appreciation. Ironically enough, if it hadn't been for the privacy afforded to her by this room, and the luxury of the iPhone, she would never have been able to organize her escape with Ali. Bakhtawara flipped Zarghoona's toshak, unstitched its cloth, and carefully picked through its cotton. Then, one by one, she opened the many drawers of Zarghoona's dresser, recently purchased by Atal's mother, and scoured through hijabs, smocks, underwear, and the old Punjabi outfits she had left behind. She gathered Zarghoona's medical textbooks and her journals, flipping through the pages, hoping to find some secret code but seeing only notes upon notes on anatomy, physiology, and disease. What a shame, Bakhtawara thought. It wasn't just her family she had given up but her future too. Where would she study now? Floating past one sea or another with a book in her hand and a pen in her mouth? Ali was a moron. But what a pretty moron. And kind too. Atal was large and sad and not very pretty. He worked in his mother's shop and (Shireen had whispered) was on the brink of dropping out of college. He seemed to be a slave of his mother, and such men—Bakhtawara had learned from Miriam—could often be cruel to their wives. Tired and empty-handed, Bakhtawara lay back on her sister's toshak and wondered if Allah would punish Zarghoona for refusing to sacrifice Ali. But she couldn't fault her sister. Bakhtawara had long known that Zarghoona did not possess the soul of a martyr and would be doomed to settle for love on earth.

In America—Bakhtawara decided—she would study medicine.

.
.

Once Raheem returned from engineering school, Kareem from business, Qaleem from high school, and Rahman from the brickyard, the family ate lunch in the living room while their father watched an epic Turkish serial on low volume.

Though incredibly thin, Farhad Niazi was a perpetually sluggish man, whose body, he often complained, felt much heavier than it looked. He was a man so averse to labor that on a number of occasions his family had almost gone hungry when he couldn't manage to raise a pickax or bring down a hammer. For this reason, he felt more indebted to Rahman than anyone else.

Not wanting to immediately spoil her son's appetite, Gul Sanga waited for Rahman to take a few bites from his paraki before she made the odd decision to tell him the good news first. "Rahman," Gul Sanga said, "Bakhtawara has agreed to marry Atal."

Rahman made an involuntary sound with his throat.

"You see, Rahman Jan . . . ," Gul Sanga went on with her story, not noticing that her son was choking on potatoes and rage. Only Bakhtawara had the foresight to quickly deliver him a pitcher of water. While Rahman washed down the obstruction in his throat, his brothers rose up in arms, demanding a blood debt, but their father quickly explained that Ali's family had already offered to repay the dowry given for Zarghoona (no matter how many years it would take) and were also willing to offer their eldest daughter to Rahman, without a dowry, as soon as she came of age.

The water Rahman drank seemed to have cooled his soul. Quietly, his burning rage dissipated into a silent fantasy of wife and child and perhaps love.

"The best thing now," Gul Sanga suggested, "is to focus on Bakhtawara."

"Our savior," Rahman said, and turned to his sister.

"It's only my duty," Bakhtawara whispered into her chest, as if she meant to hide the words beneath her clothes.

"This was not *your* duty," Rahman said. "Whatever happens, whether they deny us or not, our family will be indebted to you. Believe me, Bakhtawara, you have already—"

But before Rahman could praise her further, Bakhtawara grabbed too many dishes at once, rushed off to the rice room, and waited to update Miriam on the good news. The family had come to an agreement. Now it was only a matter of convincing the suitors.

●
○

Miss Lakhta and her son Atal were so impeccably prompt in their tardiness that every time they came for dinner, Bakhtawara found she could accurately predict their arrival to within a minute or two. This night was no different. At approximately seven forty-five p.m., when Miss Lakhta, laughing monstrously, shouted from behind their aluminum gate that she was hungry and tired and wouldn't be kept out, Gul Sanga was already there (by command of Bakhtawara) to invite them inside. Miss Lakhta strolled into the Niazi residence with her son Atal and her mother-in-law, Bibi Ashak.

The women all went into one room and Atal was led into another.

Miss Lakhta was a plump, formidable woman from Laghman, who at sixteen had been married off to a young Wardaki boy from Mississippi. Now, at forty years old, she'd spent more years in the States than she had in Laghman and spoke Pashto with an unplaceable Mississippian accent. When joyous, she was a boisterous woman with a laugh so infectious, she could get a room guffawing in a matter of seconds; but when irritated, she seemed capable of war crimes. Consequently, Gul Sanga's generally intense anxiety reached a bursting point when Miss Lakhta, finishing her first cup of chai, asked for the whereabouts of her daughter-in-law.

"Well, you see," Gul Sanga began to say, but soon found that the unrelenting shame she felt for her daughter's desertion had crumbled into the realization that her eldest girl was gone forever: a fate worse than death, since she couldn't even be comforted by the hope that they would meet again in paradise.

She stopped speaking and wept into her tea.

Miss Lakhta and her mother-in-law rose up to comfort and interrogate Gul Sanga, but it was no good. She merely sobbed and recited the name of the daughter she had lost to a boy no greater than any other. Her Zarghoona. Mercifully, Shireen jumped in and with the indifference of an undertaker explained to Miss Lakhta that Zarghoona had never wanted to marry her son. From a young age, Shireen went on, Zarghoona had loved a baker from the neighborhood named Ali and for this reason had recently decided to flee with said baker. But, luckily for Miss Lakhta, their trip and their expenses would not be going to waste because her elder sister, Bakhtawara, had valiantly volunteered to marry Atal in Zarghoona's stead, which was really a great fortune, because she would not be able to find a more suitable bride on this earth, and that in spite of the shameful circumstances, it would be disastrous for her not to accept Bakhtawara's offer, as that would suddenly disrupt the delicious momentum of the odd drama that had become their lives.

Gul Sanga stopped weeping.

Bakhtawara felt that she might start.

Obviously impressed by Shireen's nerve, Miss Lakhta and her mother-in-law turned their attention to Bakhta-wara, who suddenly wished, for the first time in her life, that she had worn some eyeliner or lipstick or at the very least had plucked her eyebrows.

"She is not as pretty as the other," Miss Lakhta said. "Darker too."

"Though she *is* thicker," Bibi Ashak noted. "Taller too. Your grandkids would be giants."

"You've raised quite a trio of daughters," Miss Lakhta said.

"Of course," Gul Sanga managed to utter, "we intend to return the dowry."

What followed was a twenty-second period of such immense silence, even the men in the other room took note of it and stopped speaking.

"Atal," Miss Lakhta finally shouted.

Slightly limping, Atal approached the entrance of the living room. His mother invited him to sit down.

Standing at six feet four inches, two hundred and fifteen pounds, Atal had the lean, wide-shouldered body of a collegiate quarterback, which was what he had intended to become for many years until his right knee was shattered in a vicious pile drive of a tackle during his junior year of high school. The injury destroyed not only his gait but some part of his spirit too. Now he limped about the earth, quiet and awkward and acne scarred, perpetually uneasy in his too powerful body, which, it seemed to him, was built for violence or performance and nothing else. Even slumped and seated, he towered over his mother.

"Atal," Miss Lakhta said, "would you be willing to marry this girl instead of the other?"

Without even asking what had happened to his former fiancée, Atal took one long look at Bakhtawara, found nothing unappealing, and agreed to the match. Gul Sanga and her daughters quietly rejoiced among themselves, while Miss Lakhta was already in the midst of replanning her son's wedding. Though Bakhtawara insisted it wasn't necessary, Miss Lakhta assured the ladies that Bakhtawara would have her own set of gold and jewels and dresses too.

That night, Bakhtawara went to update Miriam. In between the long silences, when they tried very hard not to sob, the two friends lied to each other about visits, reunions, phone calls, and a prolonged friendship that would never die under the circumstances of war and diaspora.

Then they discussed the wedding night.

•
•

Over the next two days, Bakhtawara's wedding party went about selecting new dresses, jewels, and cards. Fortunately, while Zarghoona had been merciless in her demands, selecting only the most expensive and outlandish gifts (in an attempt to scare off her suitors), Bakhtawara eagerly agreed to everything Miss Lakhta and her mother suggested. It was almost irritating. She did not insist on wearing a white wedding gown. She was not sure how she wanted her makeup done or what color her dress should be or if Atal should wear a pakol or a patki. She went about the markets in Kart-e Naw, picking at this jewel or that cloth, this ring or that chador, and it seemed to her that every item she touched, no matter how impeccably polished, stained her fingers with dust. They had only enough time to reprint wedding invitations for their immediate family in Kabul, those they could conceive of trusting with their semi-secret. Hopefully, by the will of Allah, the more distant relatives and friends from the surrounding districts in Logar and Wardak and Paktia wouldn't even notice that one sister had been swapped for the other.

When they met in the night, Miriam feverishly questioned Bakhtawara about every single decision she had made that day. "You have to take these matters more seriously. You're only married once," she said, which wasn't true, of course, but Bakhtawara didn't argue. Then Miriam spoke of her own wedding with a fondness that surprised Bakhtawara. She described how handsome her husband had looked in his dark Italian business suit. She described the meticulous order with which she had chosen the arrangement of the flowers and the linens and the silverware. She described the choreographed attan her brothers had put together. She recalled how beautiful the city seemed in the twilight of dusk. She was reminiscing, becoming nostalgic, which, Bakhtawara knew, was very dangerous for Miriam.

"He had always been such an impeccable dresser," she said. "Even in his bargain shirts and trousers, he looked no less respectable than any of his superiors. You should have seen him the first time we went out for dinner, he had on this little—"

"What do you plan to wear for the ceremony?" Bakhtawara interrupted.

"I have a few things."

"I hope you don't mind, but I have a dress for you."

Miriam denied the gift eight times in a row before she gave in to the will of the bride. That night, the dress was delivered to Miriam's door. It was in the design made popular by Nabeela of Logar, a brilliant fusion of the Kochi and Punjabi styles, with the same golden pattern as the dresses to be worn by Shireen and Bakhtawara's cousins. Somehow, though there was no way Bakhtawara could have known Miriam's measurements, the dress fit perfectly, as if it had been tailored just for her.

Once, twice, three times in her bedroom, by the light of a fire the hue of cold butter, Miriam spun.

⋮

On the morning of her wedding, Bakhtawara was driven to Zarghoona's favorite salon in a yellow Corolla, to be painted and plucked by her sister's favorite hairdressers, to prepare for the ceremony at her sister's dream banquet hall, on the day her sister had selected so many months ago, it now seemed like a false memory. She wore a heavy Kochi dress of red and green and golden tassel, many mirrored, pleated a thousand and one times. Had Bakhtawara been a slighter girl, she would not have been able to carry the weight of the many folded miles of cloth with such grace and gravity.

Guided by Miss Lakhta, four different hairdressers had layered and knotted and burned Bakhtawara's long hair into an architectural feat of an updo, an elaborate minaret of glistening black hair, gently enshrouded by a translucent green veil. Miss Lakhta watched her new bride leave the most expensive salon in Kabul with the smug satisfaction of a victorious general.

In the banquet hall, there were incredulous stares and whispers and wide-eyed confusion when Bakhtawara first entered. She sat upon the bridal stage and the guests began to approach and greet and kiss her, several of them mistakenly referring to her as Zarghoona. Bakhtawara relished this . . . this sense of disappearing inside her sister's image, her memory. Sitting there upon the stage, half the room thinking she was someone else and the other half knowing she was supposed to be, Bakhtawara had never felt so alone—or so close to God. Atal sat beside her, sweaty and pale, his long legs crossed awkwardly upon their toshak. In his white kameez and patki, he held Bakhtawara's hand so gently, she kept forgetting he was even there. Earlier, as they had walked side by side into the wedding hall, Bakhtawara had held Atal's hand to guide him where he needed to go. But now, with their hands hidden behind a small display of purple flowers, Bakhtawara was oddly comforted by the cradle of his clammy palms. Between greetings and introductions, Bakhtawara whispered to Atal about who was who and what would happen next and when he should prepare to stand.

"This is your mother's khala," Bakhtawara told him as an old orange of a woman approached their stage. "You should kiss her hand."

So he did.

"This is one of my distant cousins," she went on, "just put your hand on your chest and ask about her husband's health."

So he did.

With his mother busy rushing from one side of the wedding to the other, cursing children, greeting guests, shouting at waiters, readjusting decorations, praising Allah, and pretty much running the entirety of the banquet hall, Atal had very willingly given in to the guidance of his young bride. He knew that many considered his mother to be a brash and senseless woman, but she had also single-handedly saved his father's entire family from the brink of financial ruin. Watching her succeed, time and again, where no one thought she would (in business, in courts, in marriage, in Mississippi) had led him to believe that following his mother was the safest path in life. It was his way. Since peewee football, coaches and teachers and proxy parents had directed him toward the end zone, toward the weight room, toward classes, toward graduation, and he had thrived under that direction, under playbooks and outlines and order. If his mother had loved him less, Atal often thought, he could've been a great soldier. But sitting comfortably beside his new bride, he wondered if the universe (he did not believe in God) had blessed him, again, with a shepherd.

Bakhtawara searched the crowds of guests for anyone who might have been Miriam. There were a few women in the hall still clad in burqa and she wondered if one of these ladies was her friend, and she wondered why Miriam hadn't approached her yet, and if she was ashamed or afraid or upset, if she was watching her now, her and her groom, or if she was still at home, in her room, in the dark, and she wondered if she could forgive Miriam for not coming today, for not revealing herself, and it was in the midst of this search for Miriam that Bakhtawara spotted Nabi. She almost didn't recognize him. Along with Rahman and Raheem and Kareem and Qaleem and four other boys of blood relation, who had snuck into the hall under the careful direction of Miss Lakhta, Nabi performed the attan beneath the bridal stage. His long locks oiled and combed and coiffed, his beard trimmed down to little more than a shadow, Nabi was the last of the dancers. A small man, Nabi had the slight, graceful body of a professional swordsman, and he seemed so at peace in the dance, so in tune with the rhythm of the drums, that even those who knew him had forgotten to be afraid.

For fear of catching his glance, Bakhtawara would not watch Nabi and instead watched everything else. Shireen preparing the girls for their portion of the attan; Gul Sanga whispering to her husband near a corner of the wall separating the men from the women's side of the wedding; Farhad holding Gul Sanga's one hand in both of his; Rahman, who never danced, counting his steps as he attempted to lead the attan; Miss Lakhta slapping someone else's child for tugging at the golden curtains near the entrance of the hall; someone else rushing toward Miss Lakhta for the slapping of their child; sweat-drenched waiters hurrying back and forth, navigating the tables and the guests and the children with their eyes locked on the floor; Atal's large hands, which they would both learn together (in a matter of hours) were made for love, squeezing hers as if proclaiming his existence, as if he somehow knew that his secret rival was quietly declaring an immutable love, unabashed and unashamed, with the hopeless courage of a man living to die; Zarghoona out on some road, on some pass, in love and in fear, destined to roam forever; Miriam still trapped in her compound, donning Bakhtawara's dress, sitting near the door, its lock unclasped, slightly shifted, just enough to peer out onto the road, to watch beautiful little schoolgirls in black uniforms skip and shout and run toward their homes—sometimes alone, sometimes hand in hand—with the hot wind of the city burning her flesh because the aching in her heart was not enough.

Hungry Ricky Daddy

While our apartment hovered on the brink of a four-sided civil war over a miraculous microwave I'd bought at a flea market in Fremont, my little brother's best friend, Ricky Daddy, tried to live off the food given out at student-body meetings on campus. Monday it was the PSA, Tuesday the ASA, Wednesday the PSU, and Thursday the ASU. Every Friday, the brothers from Davis got together after jummah for free pizza in the quad. See, Ricky Daddy (whose real name was Abubakr Salem) was saving up to buy an engagement ring for a Palestinian hijabi who'd barely spoken a sentence to him—not for his lack of trying—because the second or the third intifada had left her heart immune to the temptations of his chiseled upper body.

Not that there was anything wrong with our Ricky.

He seemed to us quite lovable.

With all the looks and charm of your average Pashtun fuck boy and the pure-hearted grace of an orphaned virgin. And even though, at first, we didn't believe the fact of his virginity—what with those curls, muscles, dimples—he swore to his celibacy often and without shame. It was more than his looks, though, that made us doubt him. We used to memorize his Instagram DMs as if they were verses from the Quran. One-liners. Witty comebacks. Emoji game like Jordan.

All of that, and we were supposed to believe the kid still had his V-card at twenty-one?

But my little brother, Mahmood, swore that if Ricky's dick ever got wet, he'd know about it. We'd all know about it because Ricky couldn't lie if you made him say "Wallah."

We demanded a demonstration. The ten of us gathered in the kitchen and asked Ricky when was the last time he jerked off.

"I don't jerk off." He blushed.

"Say Wallah," we said.

He couldn't.

"Say Wallah you haven't jerked off in the past week."

He couldn't.

"Say Wallah you haven't jerked off today."

"Please stop," he said.

So, we did, but only because we loved him.

Even convinced of his virginity, we still couldn't figure out *why* exactly he wouldn't give up that dick. My brother—who'd switched to psychology to up his GPA for med school—explained that before Ricky's grandma died, she used to harp on Ricky nonstop about his dick and balls rotting away in the seventh level of Jahannam saved exclusively for zina. We felt content with that explanation and accepted him as he came.

Our Ricky Daddy.

Virgin fuck boy.

Despite his purity, Ricky's looks and his Instagram fame gave him a bad rep among the Good Girls on campus. That was why we thought Ricky had no chance with Nabeela. Though, to be honest, we didn't know if you could call Nabeela a *Good* Girl per se. I mean, she was on her deen and everything: roamed about campus (first year of her PhD in Islamic jurisprudence) head to toe in these dark outfits that revealed only her face—handsome but pale and bare—and her hands and her ballerina slippers.

She prayed fard, sunna, nafl, everything. But we were pretty sure the girl was on like six different watch lists. She had an in with the Marxists, the anarchists, the Islamists, and might have been connected to Hamas back in Palestine. Because the FBI almost certainly had a tail on her, she kept a low profile online. No FB, Twitter, Instagram (where Ricky thrived), or even a Tumblr. Besides her revolutionary habits, there was also a rumor spreading among the Arab sisters that she already had a man waiting for her in Gaza. A cousin of hers. A rebel.

We explained this all to Ricky, but he laughed it off.

"Rebels die young," he joked. "Once he's gone, I'll swoop."

"But why swoop?" we asked. "Why her? She's four years older, three inches taller, and about a hundred IQ points smarter."

Ricky didn't say anything. He just smiled that way he did: his lips sort of parted, almost pouting, but his teeth still hidden.

●
○

Our apartment had its own problems. See, there were three rooms in our place. Me and my brother and Ricky stayed in one room because we were all from Logar, none of us snored at night, and neither of them bothered me when I made dhikr or read Quran. Usually, Ricky would be quietly coding or texting while Mahmood overstudied for exams he would almost certainly pass.

Our three Arab buddies—Abed the Egyptian, Ikram the Syrian, and Yassin the Palestinian—stayed in their own room. As kids, they'd all gone to Masjid Annur together. Yassin was a bodybuilder who tried to make up for his fluffy eyebrows with stacks of muscles. He wanted to crush Israel between his bicep and his forearm. Ikram was an imam's kid. A former Qari addicted to kush. Each puff was another verse forgotten. Abed was like eight different people. He wanted everyone on campus (hippies, Nazis, Sufis, Salafists, Zionists, soldiers, frat boys) to love him. He did backflips at parties for no reason.

Three Pashtuns stayed in the third room. Two of them were twins on wrestling scholarships. They wore matching muscle shirts and skinny jeans, and whenever they went out for beers, they would come back in the night and get into fistfights over girls they'd claimed at bars. Zalmay was the third Pashtun. A Kandari from Stockton, he kept a shotgun in his closet, filmed the Twins' fight every night, and uploaded these videos on YouTube for the ad money. Twins didn't even know.

Faheem (an Indian kid from Elk Grove) shared the living room with Haydar the Kashmiri. Their rooms were sectioned off with curtains and they paid less rent than everyone else. While Faheem stayed up all night listening to Ahmed Deedat and watching *Gilmore Girls,* Haydar worked on his rap album. They usually slept in the morning and got along pretty well because Haydar had a talent for ignoring Faheem's Islamic lectures and the whispering that emitted from his curtains whenever he phoned the white girl who was not his girlfriend. That was, until the day Faheem brought the rabbit. He tried to sneak it in at night without telling anyone, but because the rabbit stayed in his room (or so we thought), no one bothered him about it. We all acted like the rabbit didn't exist, ignoring the shadow of its cage, the carrots in the fridge, the munching and squeaking and pooping. But then one morning Haydar woke up with flea bites running up and down his leg. When he asked Faheem if his rabbit had fleas, Faheem responded with a thirty-minute story about how the Prophet loved animals. Haydar, like always, let it go, but when the rest of us heard what had happened, we demanded an apartment meeting, which Faheem avoided for two weeks straight by hiding out at his cousin's place until we ambushed him at two in the morning as he was coming back to microwave some frozen daal.

———

The Twins put him in a headlock for five minutes before he admitted that the rabbit was in his car. Zalmay broke in, stole the cage, and hauled it away to Stockton.

No one ever saw it again.

After that, Faheem began to treat Haydar like shit. Wouldn't say salaam to him, wouldn't lecture him, threw out his food on purpose, complained about his raps, woke up early in the morning to watch reruns of *Ninja Warrior* on full blast. Then, inch by inch, Faheem began to move his curtain into Haydar's side of the living room. Within a month, his room was about a foot wider than it had been. Haydar called an apartment meeting and showed us photos documenting the gradual extension of Faheem's curtains. He showed us the indentations in the carpet from where his dresser was moved ten inches to the right. He showed us the bookshelf at the end of Faheem's bed that would never have fit at the beginning of the semester. He showed us the little holes in the wall where his rod used to hang. Haydar wanted his foot of space back. Faheem denied its existence.

They both demanded a vote.

Haydar had me, my brother, and two of the Arabs on his side. But the Twins voted for Faheem because he was a TA in one of their Intro to Ethics courses. Zalmay, by default, also went with the Twins, and so did Ikram, who never liked Haydar because he was a Shia. It was five vs. five. We needed Ricky to break the tie.

But Ricky was busy.

Having switched up his strategy with Nabeela, Ricky had started attending any event he thought she might show up at: Marxist book clubs, SJP meetings, anti-police rallies, postcolonial theory courses. The plan was to prove himself during meetings and classes so that Nabeela would see he wasn't a spy. Problem was he didn't know shit about anything. Hadn't read through a whole book since *Charlotte's Web* in grade school. And yet, to our surprise, Ricky Daddy began frequenting the library. At first, he was mostly there on his laptop, reading Wikipedia articles and watching ten-minute YouTube documentaries about Palestine. He examined illustrated diagrams and sketch animations of Israeli land grabs and settlement extensions. He watched street executions and cell phone clips from the bombings in Gaza. He consumed as much of the internet info as he could, until, eventually, he had to move on to real books.

●

About a month into our apartment war—with Faheem still gradually eating into Haydar's space—my little brother decided to punish the opposition by confiscating our shared microwave. That's when shit really escalated. I'd bought the microwave for fifteen bucks at a flea market in Fremont, just hoping to nuke leftover Kabuli, but the radiation didn't just heat the food, it somehow made it tastier. Wallah, all you had to do was hit Popcorn for any item and wait seven minutes for your faith in Allah's providence to be restored. I could nuke a week-old slice of pizza and the thing would taste better than it had fresh. Everyone in the apartment knew the microwave was a godsend, something like a miracle, so when Mahmood up and stole it away, our opposition sort of lost it.

The night the Twins returned to find the microwave missing, they almost wept. Thought we'd been robbed. When they figured out my brother had stolen the microwave, they tried to break into our room. We had to use a dresser as a blockade. Then Zalmay, hearing the commotion and the horrific news, brought out his shotgun and aimed at our door. Not wanting to harm the microwave, the Twins leapt at Zalmay just as he fired, pushing his shotgun toward the Arabs, who were all passed out inside their room. The shotgun pellets shattered their door. Zalmay fled. The Arabs attacked the Twins. There was a tussle in the living room and Haydar's curtains were torn, his laptop smashed, and his pleading ignored. Eventually, the Twins got Ikram and Abed into arm bars and tied them up with Haydar's curtains and dragged them to the student clinic just before the cops arrived and beat the shit out of the Somalian brothers who lived next door. Poor guys got arrested. Me and Mahmood stayed hidden all night and the next day, too, until we managed to sneak out toward dark and took refuge in Ricky's fort of books on the sixth floor of the library.

Mahmood brought the microwave along.

Ricky looked like shit. His curls were a mess. He had eye bags and yellow teeth. He was failing three of his CS classes. And he wouldn't shut the hell up about Palestine. He told us about the Ottomans and the Nakba and the Deir Yassin massacre. He told us about the PLO and the Six-Day War. He showed us on a map the borders of the apartheid wall, the locations of military checkpoints, and how the Israelis had separated Gaza and the West Bank like orphaned siblings. He told us about the Brotherhood, the intifada, the birth of Hamas, and the Oslo Accords. He read us recipes for mansaf, maqluba, and musakhan. He told us about the capture of Leila Khaled, the assassinations of Yassin and Rantisi (both killed by hellfire missiles), and the odd journey of Sheikh Abdullah Azzam. He went on and on, well into the night, drawing from this book and that, reading us quotes, showing us pictures, bodies, massacres, walls, olive trees. We fell asleep to his reading poems in Arabic.

By next morning, I'd forgotten everything he tried to teach me and went off to class. Later that night, my brother and I returned to Ricky's den for shelter, only to find him researching university appeals cases on his laptop. Apparently, Nabeela was getting expelled. An article in the *Vanguard* reported that she was filmed making anti-Semitic remarks when IDF veterans tried to disrupt a speech the SJP had organized in the quad after an eight-year-old girl was run over by settlers in Nablus. A shouting match turned into a fistfight turned into a brawl. The video was all over the internet. Toward the end of the blurred clip, someone who might've been Nabeela shouted in Arabic: "May Allah destroy the Israelis." Her hearing was set for next month. But just a few days after the brawl, Nabeela disappeared.

Back in Palestine, we heard, to marry that cousin of hers.

When we told Ricky, instead of sobbing as we thought he would, he was all questions. Who was the cousin? When

:ah? Where would they stay? What would hap-
volution?

We didn't have those answers, but Yassin probably would.

We messaged him on Facebook, and he left us on seen until we offered the microwave in exchange for his intel. Our phones dinged like wind chimes. Yassin had spoken to his sister, who had spoken to her aunt in Jerusalem, who had found out that Nabeela's cousin's name was Yusuf, that he was with the Islamic Revival, that he was locked up (without charge) in an Israeli prison, and that, in fact, he'd just started a hunger strike about six days earlier to be officially charged with a crime. Nabeela and Yusuf were set to be wed after his release, but until then, she would wait for her fiancé in the West Bank.

"The West Bank?" Ricky asked.

We showed him the messages again, expecting him to wallow, to bleed. Instead, the very next day, Ricky left the library, ordered three shawarma platters at Sam's restaurant, and announced his very own hunger strike during lunch.

The strike began in our apartment, at the start of the winter break, when all our roommates except Faheem had gone home. We made a YouTube video announcing Ricky's intention to starve his body until Yusuf Mohammad was charged with a crime. He read a verse from the Quran, condemned the crimes of Israel and the US, lay down on an old toshak, and began to starve. We posted about the strike all over Facebook and Twitter and Instagram and waited. At first, nothing much happened. I suppose people thought Ricky might have been bluffing. But around the third day of his strike, when the hunger pangs and stomach cramps got so bad for Ricky we thought he might give up, the Palestinian sisters started coming by, thanking Ricky for his bravery and snapping photos of his hunger. The pain in his face seemed to disappear into his dimples.

About six days in, word started really spreading and students from the MSA and ASA came to try to convince Ricky to stop, while students from the SJP and ASU came to argue with those who came to convince him to stop. From time to time, distant relatives (we guessed) from the East Coast came to visit too. They entered his room, muttered for a while, and left dejected. Though none of them could have known about Nabeela, each ama or khala or cousin made a passing remark about the folly of love. We didn't see them again. Then a reporter from the *Vanguard* came to do a story: "Afghan Student Starves to Free Palestinian Terrorist." Three days after that, someone left a pig carcass in our parking lot.

•
•

Ricky's muscles started melting two weeks into the strike. The pangs in his belly had stopped altogether and he felt nauseated and numb all the time. A few days later, a local news channel gave Ricky an interview. Our original YouTube video was buzzing and the article from the *Vanguard* spread from blog to blog. Supporters and haters gathered in our parking lot. They had protests and demonstrations and fistfights. Eventually, there were maybe twenty students staying in our apartment at all times, looking after Ricky. Even our roommates came home early. Yassin (premed) checked Ricky's pulse, Ikram read him Quran, the Twins carried him from bed to bathroom, Zalmay called up some of his buddies from Stockton for security, Haydar bought him a two-hundred-dollar pillow, Abed did backflips, and me and Mahmood were the only ones he'd let wash him. He was getting weaker by the day. Light-headed and slow, he couldn't stand up so easily anymore. When I rubbed his arms or his chest with a washcloth, I thought his skin would tear free. Around the end of the third week, cops and doctors from the university hospital arrived at our place, demanding that Ricky eat, ready to force-feed him with medical equipment the CIA used on prisoners in Guantánamo, but Ricky's followers all locked arms in front of our parking lot, and then our apartment, and then the door of our room, shoulder to shoulder, leaving no inch of space for the cops to pass through. They maced and beat a few of us, but we held strong for our Ricky.

Then, on the twenty-sixth day of Ricky's hunger strike, Mahmood secretly checked up on Ricky's resurrected Facebook page (ten thousand–plus followers since the strike) when he saw a message request from an account without a picture that was just called "Sister Filastin." He would've immediately ignored it if the message had not started out by calling Ricky "Abubakr Salem." At first, Ricky was upset about the secret Facebook account, but his temper quickly faded when he realized who had messaged him. He smiled—first time in a week—and started doing what he did best. For five hours straight, when he should have been reciting Quran or making dhikr or contemplating the transient nature of the mortal body, Ricky texted Nabeela. At the end of the day, Ricky asked Mahmood to delete all his old photos and posts on Instagram, FB, Twitter, and even Myspace.

"After that," he went on, "bring me a camera and link me up to a live feed."

"All right, Ricky," we said without question.

"And don't call me Ricky anymore," he said. "My name is Abubakr Salem."

•

Before we set up the live feed, we combed his hair and his beard, which now reached past his Adam's apple, and we washed his face and moisturized his lips (his vanity still breathing), and we got him ready to face the whole world just beneath the open window of our dingy little apartment room. The speech he read was not his own. Nabeela had sent it to him bit by bit on Messenger just hours before.

"Americans," it began, "my name is Nabeela Mohammad, wife of Yusuf Mohammad, who has been on a hunger strike for five consecutive weeks. On his body is a medical device connected to a surveillance room operating twenty-four hours a day. His heartbeats are slow and may stop at any moment, and doctors, officials, and intelligence officers sit on every side of him, waiting for his end. I chose to speak to you: intellectuals, writers, lawyers, journalists, and civil society activists. I invite you to visit my husband and see how he hungers.

"Americans," it went on, "you may feel the impulse to write a story about my husband. You could write, for example, of his melting flesh, of his bared rib cage, and of his stuttering breath. You could write of his eyes that no longer belong to him. And after you write the story, you may publish it and add it to your curricula, and when hundreds of your students read it, they will believe that the Palestinian dies of hunger romantically, fanatically, and without sense, and you would then rejoice in this funerary ritual and in your cultural and moral superiority. But my husband was arrested and imprisoned without charge because it is the military that rules our lands—and yours—and the intelligence apparatus that decides, and all the other components of society merely sit from a distance and watch so as to avoid the explosion of our criminal bones. For I have not heard one of you interfere to stop the loud wail of death and the quiet torture of our dark bodies. It is as if every one of you has turned into grave diggers, and everyone wears his military suit—the judge, the writer, the journalist, the merchant, the academic, and the poet— and I cannot believe that a whole society was turned into guards over our deaths and our lives. Nonetheless, you may be sure, all of you hearing this, that we will die satisfied and having satisfied. We do not accept being deported from our lands. We do not accept your courts and your laws. If you have passed over our country and destroyed it in the name of a God or a principle, you will not pass over our elegant souls, which have declared disobedience. For the defeated will not remain defeated, and the victor will not remain a victor. History isn't only ever measured by battles and massacres and prisons, but also by the incremental blood drip of the thinnest veins. A'udhu billahi min ash Shaytanir Rajim. Bismillah ir-Rahman ir-Rahim."

Then we cut the feed and posted everywhere and waited.

●

The video barely made a blip. The outrage over last month's police harassment had subsided after a boat of frat boys went missing somewhere along the Los Angeles coast. Abubakr wallowed in obscurity. His body had shrunk, and he grew more reserved in his suffering. We couldn't seem to get through to him. It was like we were watching him float away but inside himself. Our food began to taste like dirt, and our lives felt unforgivably stupid in the wake of his misery. We couldn't take it anymore. We joined the strike. First it was me and Mahmood. Then Yassin and Ikram. Then Abed and the Pashtuns. Then Haydar. Word got around, and by the time Abubakr Salem started losing his memory, we had over a hundred Muslims starving with us across Davis and Sacramento. We began buzzing online again, and our movement turned statewide. We had Muslims and Arab students from all the UCs and CSUs joining the strike. By the forty-first day, when he couldn't stop vomiting bile or shitting soft splatters of blood, our movement had become national. West Coast, East Coast, until, around six weeks in, we had organizations in the UK and France striking with us too. A Syrian artist in Belgium took a still of Abubakr Salem's face from the video of Nabeela's speech, sepia-toned it with an app, and put the image on a poster. The next day, people were wearing T-shirts and sweaters with Abubakr's starving face plastered across it.

He still looked pretty then.

On the fifty-second day of Abubakr's hunger strike, bloody sores grew out of his back and swelled and burst open like hungry mouths. His beard and his curls had grown long and wild, and he seemed to go blind from time to time. Even though our apartment had been turned into a makeshift clinic, with two or three doctors visiting us each day, we got so desperate to keep Abubakr alive, we began to microwave the five cups of chai he drank after each of the daily prayers, hoping its magic might keep his heart beating. If he closed his eyes for too long and stopped chanting bismillah, we would rush to his side and hold a mirror to his lips and wait for him to open one eye and joke: "Is that me in there?"

Through it all—the vomiting and shitting and lapses in consciousness—Abubakr kept on texting Nabeela about God knows what because he could not let us see and would not let us type, though his fingers seemed to be on the brink of breaking.

.
.

Two months into our ordeal, Faheem finally joined the strike. About five minutes after that, so did the white girl who was not his girlfriend. A few hours later, CNN came to interview her. By that night, she had become a worldwide sensation. The next morning, Trump flew to Tel Aviv and personally requested that Netanyahu officially charge Yusuf Mohammad with a crime. So, after sixty-eight days on strike, Yusuf Mohammad was formally charged with inciting violence because his protest had caused several riots in Gaza. He was moved to a different facility, and with his left wrist still handcuffed to a hospital bed, Yusuf Mohammad, spokesman for the Islamic Revival, graduate student, poet, orphan, and husband, ended his fast with a date and a glass of milk, before promptly dying of heart failure.

Almost exactly ten hours later, Abubakr Salem, formerly known as Ricky Daddy, ate a microwaved date, drank a cold glass of milk, typed a message to Nabeela, and stopped starving.

•
•

My roommates and I were the ones who washed Ricky for the janaza. He had no other family. Me and Mahmood did the istinja while the rest of the guys helped with wudhu. Only Faheem could not bring himself to touch Ricky's body, and so, instead, he kept filling our plastic water jug with hundreds of flower petals. Three times we washed his body with lotus water and camphor, and then we trimmed his beard and cut his hair and brushed his teeth and cleaned his sores until his stench of death was smothered by tree bark and flower petals.

Before the strike, Ricky once told us a story about

Sheikh Abdullah Azzam, who was killed in a car bomb in Peshawar but whose body—it was said—was left without any mark or wound or blemish. And it wasn't that I expected Ricky's sores and bruises to disappear with his dying, but after he died, and we wrapped his body in a kafan, I wanted so badly for his corpse to be perfect again that I could not bring myself to say the dua for the dead during his burial. In the end, he was so light I swear to Allah I could have carried him the fifteen miles from the mosque to the grave by myself. I would have done it, too, had my roommates let me.

Two days after Ricky died, I messaged Nabeela's secret Facebook account, and for whatever reason—maybe she thought Ricky's account had been hacked, maybe she just didn't want to hear from me—she never replied. Seven months later, Nabeela gave birth to a daughter in Bethlehem. Story went that just before the hunger strike started, she was able to smuggle Yusuf's sperm out of the prison in a disinfected candy wrapper. She never went on to marry. She took up her husband's former position as spokesman for the Islamic Revival, and due to the public nature of his death, and her daughter's birth, and her speeches, which became more striking with her accumulated years of suffering, and her habit of always wearing the full niqab so that almost no one on earth knew what she looked like, Nabeela became a sort of icon. She organized the most devastating series of bombings in Jerusalem's history, her speeches and writings were collected into an award-winning book of essays, and after assisting in the Islamic Revival's takeover of the West Bank, which some say was orchestrated through the compliance of the IDF, she began her own splinter organization. Her followers worshipped her and swore by her immortality, though there were reports she had been assassinated by Mossad and that it was actually her daughter who had taken up her niqab and her position as the secret face of the Palestinian Islamist resistance.

We never believed the rumors of her dying.

In fact, over the years of her increasing fame, at one point or another, each of us from Ricky's apartment tried to contact Nabeela in order to declare our love and offer our lives. We swore to be gentle husbands or loyal soldiers, and none of us ever married anyone else (except for Faheem). Instead, I graduated from Davis, sought solitude at Zaytuna, lost faith in the white Sufis, went to Turkey, got caught up in the civil war, came back to the States, was arrested for funding terrorism, tried to travel to Palestine, was denied entry, and eventually ended up in Afghanistan. In that time, I sent Nabeela so many messages and letters and asked her so many stupid questions, I never thought she would read them. I asked, for example, if she loved Yusuf and if Yusuf loved her, and if she loved him, what was it she loved? I asked her who he was and what he read. I asked her if her daughter was the Second Coming of Christom. I asked her if she ever watched the video of Ricky giving her speech. I asked her if she noticed how he'd combed his hair and brushed his beard. I asked her what she thought of the way he spoke her words. I asked her if she might let Ricky take her out on a date in Jannah after we all died. I asked her what Palestine looked like. I told her I imagined many rolling hills and olive trees and roads built of white stone.

"I thought he looked very beautiful," Nabeela replied one morning, some years after Ricky died, and then asked me who had moistened his lips.

Saba's Story

About a month before our Agha flew back to his old village in Logar, he demanded that one of his three sons—preferably whichever one of us loved and respected him the most—buy him a metal detector. I tried to dissuade him, but Agha's one of those OG Pashtuns who'd argue with Allah over the nature of existence.

He went on to explain his intentions with a story.

"Some seventy years ago," he started, "after Logar was invaded by the English, many of the villagers in our kaleh fled through the Black Mountains for safety. Your Nikeh was guiding one of these groups of refugees when an English regiment suddenly fell upon them. A massacre ensued, and only Nikeh was able to escape into a series of caves and underground tunnels, which led him so deep into the heart of the Black Mountains, he became hopelessly lost.

"For several days, he wandered these tunnels, without food, without water, without knowing in which direction he should pray, without even being sure that God could hear him so deep within the black stone. Eventually, just as he was on the verge of collapsing from thirst, your Nikeh came upon a secret city within the mountains. A city of gold and jewels, of statues and idols and other remnants of the Kafir fire lovers from which we descended. He gathered as much of the treasure as he could and restarted his journey out of the caves. But, again, he became so lost and weak that, one by one, he dropped every jewel he carried, giving them up to Allah in the hope that He might free him in return. A few hours later, Nikeh escaped the mountain with only a single golden nugget shoved so far up his colon he supposed even Allah couldn't see it.

"Your Nikeh buried the nugget somewhere on our land, and for many years I thought your kaka used the gold to pay off the caseworker who got us into America in '82, but he called me the other day wanting to make amends. I brought up the gold, and he said there was no gold. You boys understand?"

We did. A hundred times over.

This was Agha's latest attempt in a series of get-rich-quick schemes. Though Agha had always been wary of schemers—he had seen himself, for a long time, as a worker's worker—after he was injured in a trucking accident, and after the nerves in his neck and shoulder got torn up, leaving his hands almost useless, and after his company denied him workers' comp, and after Medi-Cal refused to cover his pain meds, my family suddenly found itself without a steady source of income. Agha took his bosses to court for the comp, but the judges saw it their way. We found ourselves in debt.

So while he wallowed in his depression, his nerve damage, and his insomnia, Agha started coming up with a never-ending series of schemes to get us out of the red: buying salvaged scrapers and trying to hustle them on craigslist or growing gandana in the backyard and selling bushels at the mosque or looking to flip land. Everywhere a lot popped up in Sac, he was there bidding with money he didn't have and wouldn't have and could barely dream about.

When my two little brothers and I explained to Agha

that a halfway decent metal detector was going to cost about a hundred and fifty bucks on Amazon, and that the girls needed backpacks for the first day of school, and that the garage door was still busted, and that Athai's walker got stolen, and that my FAFSA was delayed, and that there were a hundred other little things we could use the money for, he asked us how long the delivery might take.

Both of my brothers DM'd me at the same time. They demanded that I shut his scheme down like I had with Operation Chicken Coop just a few days ago. But two rejections in one week seemed like two too many. Besides, he was in such a good mood.

I bought the metal detector.

About a month later, Agha was on a plane to Afghanistan, hoping to scour, but also to reclaim, a few portions of his father's land. Upon arriving in Kabul, he and his nephew Waseem (a banker, an orphan, and a genuine sweetheart) planned to secretly drive out to our old village in Logar. Apparently, fighting between the marines, the government forces, and the Ts had escalated rapidly in Logar. Ts were retaking territory. The Afghan army was panicking. Marines couldn't figure who to shoot. Pit stops led to executions. And bandits were thriving.

If the wrong Logari got word of Agha's return, some

desperate gunmen might try to see if he could get a taste
of that American money he was supposed to be harboring.
Alhamdulillah, though, Agha arrived at his father's compound alive and well. Malang (Agha's hash-headed cousin
who watched over our land) greeted him at the inner gate
and quietly led him to the quarters of his compound that
were slowly being taken over by old Masoomai—the scourge.
According to Agha, old Masoomai was related to our family through a marriage that never should have occurred in
the first place.

Story went that back in the 1970s, Agha had an older
half-sister named Saba, who was beset early in her teens by
rumors questioning her purity, and although the rumors
were never confirmed with a pregnancy or a confession, they
ruined her reputation, and Saba entered her twenties without a single suitor to her name. As a result, our Nikeh felt
obliged to give his daughter to old Masoomai, a little slug
of a man twenty years her elder, who had recently inherited
his dead brother's land. For a time, Masoomai was very well-
off, with crops and revenue streams aplenty, but about a
year into the marriage, the Soviets invaded, and his entire
compound was obliterated in a Russian bombing. He fled
to his wife's house, seeking sanctuary, and out of the kindness of his heart (Agha claimed) our Nikeh let Masoomai

live on a small parcel of land that he might've one day given to Saba. It was supposed to be a temporary situation, but over the next two years, as Nikeh and the rest of his sons were killed or jailed or forced to flee the war, Masoomai stayed on in Logar. Not even his wife's martyrdom—poor Saba Shaheed was killed in one of Dostum's bombings, atop her only child, whose life she saved with her death— could persuade him to leave. Then, after assuming his dead wife's claim over the land, Masoomai remarried and began to repopulate Nikeh's compound. Over the next three decades, Masoomai's many sons and then grandsons grew older and stronger, some of them becoming Ts, others joining the ANA, until they gradually swallowed up larger and larger portions of Agha's compound. But in spite of the strength of Masoomai's many sons, Agha wasn't ready to concede his birthright. In particular, there was an unspoken dispute regarding an orchard of apple trees on the western side of the compound, which also happened to be the portion of the land where Agha thought Nikeh might have buried his stolen treasure.

The next night, we got a call from Logar at one in the morning. Mor answered. It was Agha. He was calling from the orchard. When Mor saw me enter the kitchen, she shoved the phone into my hands.

———

"Marwand," Agha shouted through the speaker, "I need you to get a ticket to Logar as soon as possible. You understand? I'll explain the whole story later. Just go to the Singhs' shop, buy a disposable phone, and give me a missed call. I'll contact you as soon as I can."

Mor stood in the kitchen and watched me closely. Her hair was uncovered and fell down to her waist in a mess of curls. Usually Athai—our Agha's mom—wanted Mor to maintain her purdah even in the house. How Mor managed to keep all those curls hidden in her hijab was always a mystery to me.

"Gather the cash," he went on, "buy the ticket, and whatever you do, don't tell your Mor."

As soon as I hung up, I told Mor.

It took her exactly three phone calls to figure out what had happened. Malang's wife was the one with the story. Apparently, while Agha was scouring the grounds of his orchard, determined to locate his father's lost treasure, he accidentally dug up an old green parrot mine instead. Agha didn't touch the Soviet artifact, and he didn't want anyone else to touch it either. He covered the mine with a thin dusmal, sat nearby to keep watch, and refused to leave the orchard.

After Mor told me the story Malang's wife told her, we

discussed how we might get the money for the ticket. That was when Athai walked into the kitchen, complaining of a bad dream she'd had about her only living son, pretending that she hadn't been listening in on our conversation. She was a small woman who resembled a very large kofta. She asked us if anything had happened to her boy whom she loved and raised and would die for. So I told her the truth. She evoked Allah's mercy and asked us what we were going to do.

The plan went like this:

Mor would gather her funds: savings from babysitting, seamstressing, gandana selling, and the occasional catering job. For a long time, Agha had forbidden Mor from working, but when we lost the trial, some stubborn vein in him withered, and now she was the one keeping our shipwrecked finances afloat. After calling a few customers who owed her money—mostly Kabuli women who looked down on her because she never finished high school or because she wore the chador everywhere she went or because she'd never cashed a check in her life—she said she could gather a thousand by the end of the day. My little brothers and I pooled our earnings too. We worked side jobs when we weren't studying. I was slowly killing myself at a fireworks warehouse and both of my brothers worked in a shawarma shop with the Kandahari New Yorkers. All in all, we added another thousand to the pot. But while two thousand was enough to purchase a ticket on short notice, Mor told me I'd need some pocket change to bribe officials and family members. I sought out Athai. She had two hundred and sixty-three dollars stuffed into a secret pocket in her mattress. She didn't think we knew.

Just as we got all the cash together, counted it out, and contacted Pamir Travel about finding me a ticket, Agha called me back on the disposable phone.

"Marwand," he said, "did you buy the ticket yet?"

"Just got off the phone with Pamir."

"Call back and cancel."

"But they said no refunds, Agha."

"Tell your Mor. She'll get the refund."

Mor made a call to my ama who made a call to a friend who made a call to an aunt who made a call to her sister-in-law who knew Mr. Pamir's mother-in-law who got us the refund.

"We're going to need that money for something else," Agha said, and went on to explain his intentions with a story.

"Just after Fajr," he started, "I climbed down into the pit of our orchard with my metal detector and for almost six hours I searched the grounds, inch by inch, finding shit. Then just as I was getting near the edge of the orchard's wall, I heard the first beep-beep of the detector. In a rush I cut into the earth and almost didn't see the green parrot mine sticking up out of the dirt. It might have been a dud, but I couldn't be sure. So before anything else, I wanted to talk to you. I told Malang's kid to tell Malang to tell Waseem to get me a cell. It was only when I heard your voice that I knew I needed to see you in person. I couldn't help it. I'm sorry."

My Agha didn't apologize much for anything.

He went on: "While I waited for you to arrive, I watched over the mine to make sure no one discovered or reported it. Masoomai's grandkids thought the orchard belonged to them and wanted to play in the trees. I barked most of them away, but one of his granddaughters and her little mute brother wouldn't leave me alone. She was maybe twelve. They looked down on me from the road above the pit of the orchard and the girl asked me what I was doing. When I told her I was planting a tree, she left and then came back ten minutes later, asking me why I hadn't made any progress. I told her I was tired. So she left again and returned with a platter of tea and cookies. I howled for her not to come down and I kept on howling as she walked up to the edge of the orchard, climbed down an apple tree with one hand, and crept toward the spot where I had dug up the mine.

"She glanced at the dusmal, didn't say a word, and set the tea down near my feet. Though I didn't want to reward her efforts, I was parched and the tea was quite good. She sat a few feet away from me. I told her that Logari girls listened to their elders. So she recited the hadith about the prostitute that gave water to a thirsty dog.

"'So I'm a dog?' I asked her.

"'If you're a dog, what does that make me?' she said quickly and without smiling.

"'What's your name?'

"'Saba,' she said.

"Turned out she was Saba Shaheed's only granddaughter. Little Saba's parents died years ago in an American bombing. That was when her brother, Zalmay, stopped speaking. Masoomai took them both in, knowing that Zalmay and little Saba would have the strongest claim to Saba Shaheed's land. It took me awhile to picture my sister's face, but there it was in little Saba. The same big eyes, little nose, skin like shir chai. Because little Saba would not leave, we chatted for a while. She asked me about America, and I asked her about Logar. Zalmay came down too. To communicate, he pressed his sister's hand in a certain spot, in a certain way, and then Saba translated his questions. He asked me about you and your brothers. I went on for a long time.

"At around Maghrib, little Saba went to tell Malang and his family that I was going to eat in the orchard like I used to do as a child, and then she brought me my dinner. After we ate, they promised to go back inside, but first Saba and Zalmay brought out a toshak and a heavy blanket, and they set up my bed. I slept all night without waking.

"In the morning, Saba sat across from me with the green parrot mine in her lap.

"'It's a dud,' she said, and handed me the mine.

"I inspected it. The parrot was bright green and so light, it didn't hurt my hands to hold it. Really, it never looked so much like a parrot as it did a Frisbee. I remembered that when I was a child, I used to play Frisbee in the fields in the summer. We stole the lids from the plastic containers our mothers used to store dough, and we knew they would whup us when they found out, but the games were worth it. I would run across these fields of cut wheat and make diving leaps into a dirt that would never scrape me, and I always threw the lid where the catcher would be and not where the catcher was. It was such a mysterious game. We made up all the rules as we went, and we never wrote them down.

"Afterward, I told Saba the story of how your Nikeh got lost in the mountains, and how he escaped the tunnels and then buried the golden nugget somewhere on these lands.

"'But Kaka,' she said, 'how could the gold have survived all the bombs?'

"'And the thieves?' I added.

"'Besides, Kaka, how big could the nugget have been for your father to have hidden it where he did?'

"And it was at that moment, as I was contemplating the impossible width of my dead father's asshole, that I realized you had to marry Saba."

I could hear two quick breaths over the line.

"Listen," he said, ignoring my silence, "I know there are a hundred reasons why you shouldn't marry her. I know my request is unreasonable. But a Muslim is nothing if not a believer. Thirty years ago, your Nikeh sold my half-sister to an old man because of rumors no one could confirm. Since then our family has suffered one calamity after another. The Communists, the executions, the Soviets, the bombings, the emigration, Massoud, Dostum, the other warlords, America, but here is our chance, me and you, to make it all good again. It is as if Allah had already ordained it. It is as if He is testing us. Do you understand?"

"No," I said quietly, maybe a hundred times.

He waited over the phone for me to finish. As patient as he'd ever been. Mor and Athai and my little brothers and sisters had all entered the kitchen. They watched me. Somehow, they all knew what was going on. Mor seemed very sad and Athai very happy. My brothers and sisters mostly seemed confused.

"Marwand," my father went on, "I won't force you and no one will force her. It's up to you. It's up to the both of you."

Years later, after they sent me Saba's picture, and after everyone in my family confirmed for me she was pretty, and after I spoke with her over the phone and then over the cell and then over Skype and then in person, and after we were married, and after she left Logar and came to the States, and after she told me, night after night, all the little stories that made up her life, I asked her one morning to tell me her version of the story of the parrot in the orchard.

"But your father told it beautifully," she said to me in a home, in a room, in a bed, very far away from Logar. "And why must we always ruin what is beautiful with what is true?"

Occupational Hazards

1966-1980, Shepherd, Deh-Naw, Logar

> Duties included: leading sheep to the pastures near
> the Black Mountains; counting the length between the
> shadows of chinar trees cast on dirt roads; naming
> each sheep after a prophet from the Quran, who,
> according to Maulana Nabi, were all herders of sheep
> at one point in their lives; reciting verses from the
> Quran to dispel djinn; stealing fruit from neighbors'
> orchards for no reason at all; watching sheep; counting
> sheep; loving sheep; understanding the nature of
> sheep; protecting sheep from bandits, witches, wolves,
> rapists, demons, and half-brothers: the Captain and
> the King; taking younger brother, Watak, along on

journeys to the pastures; swimming in a stream with
Watak instead of watching sheep; losing two sheep,
Dawud and Ismael; getting beaten by the Captain for
losing sheep; leaving Watak at home; never taking
eyes off the sheep again.

1969-1975, Grade School Student, Deh-Naw, Logar

Duties included: sneaking away from home on the
first day of school with half-nephews (sons of the
Captain) to sign up for classes without permission
from Hajji Alo, who says school is for Communists
and Kafir and stooges of the Crown; registering
identity with the government minister at the local
school office; existing for the first time in the official
records of King Zahir Shah's modernist regime;
begging Hajji Alo for forgiveness; walking two miles
to school, barefoot, without a notebook or a pencil
or Hajji Alo's forgiveness; learning arithmetic;
reading and writing in Farsi and Pashto; excelling
at arithmetic; fighting schoolboys for excelling at
arithmetic; fighting schoolboys for no reason at all;
fighting older boys, stronger boys, prettier boys;
earning a reputation as a brawler; earning the
nickname "Alo's Wolf"; earning Hajji Alo's forgiveness;
learning about the auspicious and honorable kings of

Afghanistan in history class; coming home from
school to discuss the auspicious and honorable kings
of Afghanistan with Hajji Alo; hearing from Hajji
Alo that almost all of the kings of Afghanistan were
traitors, sadists, cowards, pimps, traitors, servants
of the English, servants of the Iranians, servants of
the Hindus, slavers, and traitors again, except, of
course, for the honorable Mirwais Nikeh, Ahmad
Shah Baba, and Wazir Akbar Khan, may Allah (swt)
forgive them; returning to school to question the
honor of the kings of Afghanistan; arguing with
Malam Sahib: standing up before the class of fifty
boys—some of them ragged and dirty, some of
them still bleeding from rock fights in the yard, some
of them so beautiful they will be doomed to lives
of torment—hand outstretched, palm up and open,
as Malam Sahib raises his switch and cuts through
the air with a sharp whistle that will one day resemble
the distant flight of rockets; accepting the thrashes
from Malam Sahib, who is so malnourished and
whose arms are so thin and whose switch is so flimsy,
it doesn't even break skin; rubbing calloused flesh and
smiling; returning home, triumphant; bidding farewell
to the Captain, who is sent to America for military
training by King Zahir Shah.

1971-1982, Farmer, Deh-Naw, Logar

Duties included: plowing fields; scattering manure; planting corn and wheat and tomatoes and eggplant; ensuring the fair and equal distribution of water throughout the village by maintaining a series of interconnected canals extending from the Logar River; picking apples and tomatoes; shucking corn; harvesting wheat, rice, onions, potatoes, beets, carrots, and gandana; avoiding beatings from half-brothers; hiding Watak from half-brothers; teaching Watak the tricks of the plow, the hoe, the shovel, the hammer, the sickle fork, and the fist; laboring alongside Watak in the wheat fields and in the apple orchards and on the dirt roads and near the Black Mountains; watching him try to keep pace; laughing at him fail; chopping down chinar trees with Hajji Alo, ignoring Hajji Alo's calls to slow down, clearing twenty chinar trees in a day, impressing Hajji Alo; chopping twenty-five chinar trees the next day and injuring left wrist in the process; not knowing that the wrist is broken until two days later when it swells to the size of a cantaloupe; hiding the injury from Hajji Alo and continuing to work; revealing the injury to Watak, who tells Hajji Alo; receiving permission from Hajji Alo to travel to Puli Alam to see a doctor, who fashions a brace with sticks and shreds of cloth; slowly mending, healing; resting broken arm for several weeks; hearing word of the return of the Captain; climbing up into the apple trees of Hajji Alo's orchard to gaze up at the spectacle of the Captain flying an F-15 tactical fighter jet above Deh-Naw; forgetting that arm is broken and waving at the first Logari in the sky; dreaming of jets for years afterward.

1972–1976, Merchant's Assistant, Mandai, Kabul

Duties included: waiting sleeplessly for three days and three nights before the date of the trip to Kabul; accompanying Hajji Alo on the short walk to the market village of Wagh Jan, where buses from Kabul show up every few days at Fajr; tugging along a donkey strapped to the limit with goods to sell in Kabul; sitting with Hajji Alo on the steps of a shop in Wagh Jan, in the cold of the morning, wrapped up together in a shared patu; watching the headlights of the bus cascade through early morning mist; journeying from Logar to the Mandai markets in Kabul; following Hajji Alo through massive crowds of shoppers and sellers and servants and guards; observing Hajji Alo's haggling technique; learning Hajji Alo's haggling technique; haggling under the

supervision of Hajji Alo; selling wheat, corn, fat,
oil, sheep's wool, vegetables; buying flour, cloth,
linens, shoes, jackets, and chaplaks; hauling supplies;
inspecting quality of supplies; eating freshly grilled
shish kebab on the street; seeing the lights of the
shops in Kabul glimmer like fairies; catching the
second to last bus back to Logar before it departs;
resting head on Hajji Alo's wiry arm; returning
home; meeting up with Watak on the roof of the
compound in Logar in the night; retelling Hajji Alo's
stories; falling asleep together underneath the
starry sky.

1976–1978, Merchant, Mandai, Kabul

Duties included: receiving instruction from Hajji Alo
to head to Kabul with an allotment of cash (alone);
waiting in Wagh Jan (alone); journeying to Kabul
(alone); haggling with merchants (alone), purchasing
necessary supplies for at least half the asking price
(alone); sneaking into the latest Amitabh Bachchan
film (alone); hearing word of political strife amid the
Communists in Kabul (alone); cursing the Communists
in Kabul (alone); fighting a pack of college students
in Kabul (alone); barely escaping a terrible beating
(alone); rushing through streets and alleys and open

sewers (alone); staining new clothes in sewage (alone);
bathing, clothed, in the Kabul River (alone); sitting
on the edge of a bridge above the Kabul River (alone);
drying in the setting sun (alone); returning home
on the last bus out of Kabul (alone); resting head on
window of bus and dreaming it is the bony shoulder of
Hajji Alo (alone).

1976–1979, High School Student, Deh-Naw, Logar

Duties included: studying history, algebra, chemistry,
biology, English, Pashto, Farsi, Arabic, physics;
discussing communism, Marxism, Stalinism, Maoism,
Islamism, Salafism, Wahhabism, and jihad; being
forced to pledge loyalty to Daoud, then Taraki, then
Amin, then Karmal; being forced to march to the tune
of Communist chants; hearing word of purges and
coups in Kabul; hearing word of the murders of
imams and elders in Puli Alam and Baraki Barak and
other distant villages; noticing the disappearance of
dissident students and teachers at school; watching
Communist soldiers arrive in Deh-Naw in the middle
of the night to arrest the Captain for his military
training in America and his professed loyalty to
Daoud Khan; praying for the Captain to live after
years of praying for him to die.

1977-1979, Mujahid Recruit, Deh-Naw, Logar

Duties included: gathering old English rifles with
cousins and neighbors and traveling up to the Black
Mountains; meeting with mujahideen forces recently
arrived from as close as Baraki Barak and as far away
as Bamyan; guiding mujahideen fighters through the
mountains of Logar all the way on to Peshawar;
continuing to attend the high school overrun by
Communists while still secretly assisting the
mujahideen; heading to Kabul with the King to
retrieve the Captain because he has been released
by Chairman Karmal after the Soviets executed
Chairman Amin for executing Chairman Taraki;
waiting outside the prison with hundreds and
thousands of other Afghans who are searching for
their disappeared sons or brothers or fathers;
witnessing the release of only a few hundred prisoners,
the Captain, alhamdulillah, among them; journeying
back to Logar; dropping out of high school in the
twelfth grade after a failed sickle-fork ambush by
fellow students; running off to the mujahideen camps
in the Black Mountains; growing out hair and beard;
joining the forces of Maulana Mohammad Nabi;
waiting for the call to action, to ambush, to kill and
die for the sake of Allah.

1980–1981, Mujahid, Deh-Naw, Logar

Duties included: transporting a rewired Soviet bomb
that had landed in the center of Hajji Alo's compound
without exploding; avoiding Communist kill
squads and Soviet airpower; planting the rewired
Soviet bomb near the bridge above the Logar River
where Soviet patrols often cross; waiting in the
branches of a mulberry tree for the arrival of
enemies; watching a tank approach the bomb; never
seeing the bomb explode, only hearing its burst, and
smelling the stench of cooked flesh; returning home
and sniffing wheat, flowers, dirt, leaves, shit, wood,
gunpowder, anything, anything else; firing on Russian
tanks and patrols; firing and missing; firing and never
killing; surveilling the skies for Soviet helicopters on
the roof of the compound with Watak; warning family
when air raids approached; huddling in a bomb
shelter with Watak and mother and little sisters;
breathing bomb smoke and shattered earth;
carrying a rifle at all times; burying the tattered
remnants of neighbors and friends and women and
children and babies and cousins and nieces and
nephews and a beloved half-sister named Khoro;
refusing Watak his right to jihad by referring to the
twentieth hadith from the Book of Jihad in the Sunan

an-Nasa'i, because someone must live for mother and little sisters.

1982, Reaper, Deh-Naw, Logar

Duties included: heading to the fields in the dark of predawn to cut wheat and gather crops with Watak so that the family does not starve to death while waiting out the occupation; dodging Communist patrols and Soviet helicopters; hiding in stalks of grain and branches of mulberry trees as the headlights of tanks and armored trucks cascade past grain and leaves and shadow; huddling in a field with Watak; seeing a searchlight float closer and closer; hearing Watak's plan to split up and take different routes home to divert the Communists; wavering; wavering; wavering; agreeing with Watak's plan to split up; splitting up; rushing home; getting spotted by a patrol; dodging one hundred bullets and two rockets; making it home just in time to find out that Watak was caught by a patrol and executed at the bank of a canal in the shade of a mulberry tree; learning that six other family members had also been murdered; spending the entire night digging graves and collecting limbs; seeking blood; seeking death; seeking the solitude of gunfire; watching little sisters, twelve and three, search for roots in the dead garden; deciding to live, to leave; telling Hajji Alo to abandon Logar; arguing with Hajji Alo about abandoning Logar; giving up on Hajji Alo; abandoning him to his bombarded compound in Deh-Naw; gathering the rest of the family with a number of donkeys and horses; fleeing.

1982, Refugee, Peshawar, Pakistan

Duties included: traveling on horseback through the White Mountains toward Peshawar; hiding in bushes and caves and canals to avoid Communist patrols; looking after aunts, uncles, cousins, nieces, nephews, mother, and sisters; getting caught up in the middle of a firefight between Soviets and mujahideen on a trail in the desert; losing track of sisters and nieces and the King; searching on horseback for sisters and nieces and the King; hearing the echoes of sisters calling for help in the mountains where they have escaped from the King; finding sisters and nieces on a stony trail of junipers and carrying them off on horseback; coming upon the King along the way, half-mad and starving, feet bleeding, on the brink of oblivion; rescuing him too; reaching the camps in Peshawar; finding nothing but barren plains; sleeping in a dried canal; setting up tents on a deserted patch

of land; gradually building up walls of mud around
the tents; searching for work.

1982, Laborer, Peshawar, Pakistan

Duties included: cutting and hauling wheat for twelve
hours straight, 40 rupees a day; raising enough money
to hire another donkey to return to Logar to retrieve
Hajji Alo after all hope for the salvation of Deh-Naw
has been lost; finding Hajji Alo in his wreck of a home
still brandishing the ancient sword he used to chop
down English invaders during the third Anglo-Afghan
war; assuring the old man that they would return to
fight off the Soviets just as soon as the women were
settled, trekking back to the tents in Peshawar; not
knowing that Hajji Alo will never see Logar again.

1983, Stone Breaker, Hasan Abdal, Pakistan

Duties included: breaking and hauling fractured stones
from the Kirana Hills where General Zia is obliterating
mountains to build a testing facility for Pakistan's first
atomic bomb; working two weeks at a time, thirteen
hours a day, no breakfast, no lunch, only one huge
meal in the work camp at night; filling a dolly behind a
huge tractor with as many of the dynamited mountain
stones as possible; breathing dust and earth; breathing

stone and tar; never coughing, never tiring, never
hurting; turning mountains into roads; hearing word
that the Captain's military connections in America
have finally come through; flying.

1984–1989, Assembly Line, Montgomery, Alabama

Duties included: arriving in the United States without
knowing its language or laws or customs; renting a
small trailer in Mobile right beside the trailers of the
Captain and the King; finding work at an auto parts
factory along with half-brothers and half-nephews and
Korean, Chinese, Hmong, Laotian, Cambodian, and
Vietnamese immigrants; replacing local Black workers
because the white factory owner is eager to be rid of
them; assembling harness wires for Dodge, Chrysler,
and Volvo vehicles for $3.50 an hour, ten hours a day;
purchasing groceries and medication for Hajji Alo,
who at ninety-nine years old keeps asking for the
whereabouts of Watak; telling Hajji Alo he will return
home any day now; driving youngest sister to and
from grade school; keeping the fact of youngest sister's
education away from Hajji Alo; hearing word of a
community of Afghan refugees in California; tiring of
the ghosts of Alabama; saving up enough money to
buy a Chevy Astro minivan; hauling Hajji Alo and

mother and sisters across the country and leaving the
Captain and the King behind, forever.

1989–1991, Plumber's Assistant, Rycole Engineering, San Francisco, California

Duties included: renting a small apartment in
Hayward, California, across the street from another
family of Afghans; maintaining boilers in buildings
in San Francisco at $12.00 an hour; driving a 1950s
Ford F1 from work site to work site through the chilly
fog of the city by the sea; beginning citizenship
paperwork; visiting the Golden Gate Bridge with
mother and sisters but not Hajji Alo, who is
bedridden; searching for a wife in Fremont; passing
citizenship exam; failing to find a wife in Fremont;
quitting job as a plumber's assistant in order to fly
back to Pakistan to find a wife in Peshawar; roaming
through the dirt roads of the refugee camps; hearing
word of a family from Logar, old neighbors, with
eligible daughters; visiting said family with two old
aunts; meeting the girl's father, a pharmacist, once
jailed and tortured by the Communists for giving
medical aid to mujahideen; impressing the girl's father
with stories from the jihad; receiving the shireeni;
meeting fiancée for the first time in a room of flowers

and mirrors on wedding day; realizing she is only eighteen years old; promising her a good life and all her Islamic rights; going through with the nikkah; beginning the paperwork for her visa; spending a few short weeks together at her father's home; learning that she left Logar when she was only six and that she hardly remembers Afghanistan; wondering if it would have been better that way; heading back to America for more work.

1991-1992, Newspaper Deliveryman, *Hayward Daily Review*, Hayward, California

Duties included: filling the trunk and back seat of a Nissan Maxima with copies of the *Hayward Daily Review;* delivering papers from 3:00 a.m. to 6:00 a.m.; calling wife every other night with shitty phone cards that always end up eating two minutes out of every five; finding out wife is pregnant; learning that her pregnancy will delay the visa process; delivering more papers; completing wife's visa paperwork after she passes her interview at the embassy in Peshawar; quitting job as a newspaper deliveryman in order to fly back to Pakistan to pick up wife and child.

1992–1994, Rug Merchant, Caravans, San Francisco, California

Duties included: showcasing rugs; lifting two-hundred-pound rugs; cooking and cleaning for Agha Sahib, a wealthy Hazara from Kabul; coming up with absurd plans to sabotage Agha Sahib's brother and main rival, Sayeed Sahib, who owns a different rug shop one block over; hosting parties at the store; serving the legendary Ustad Mahwash; hearing her sing in person; witnessing the birth of a second son and the death of Hajji Alo; escorting Hajji Alo's body back to Peshawar, where he was born 110 years ago, the eldest son of the nomad Lahore who was the son of the nomad Sayed Akbar who was the son of the nomad Mahdat who was the son of the nomad Azmat who was the son of the nomad Shahee who died attempting to kill a tiger with his bare hands; losing job as a rug seller in the process.

1995–1999, Convenience Store Clerk, 7-Eleven, San Lorenzo, California

Duties included: riding the BART every morning to the unincorporated community of San Lorenzo; manning the cash register from 6:00 a.m. until 11:00 a.m.; heading home for an hour-long nap

before traveling back to the store from 2:00 p.m. until
11:00 p.m. for $15.00 an hour, cash; witnessing the
birth of a third son; watching older sons ransack the
store with almost total abandon; watching youngest
sister graduate from San Lorenzo High School; paying
for her books and fees at the University of California,
Davis; getting robbed at gunpoint four times in one
year; receiving a tip that a tax on tobacco will raise
the cost of cigarette packs across the state; buying
$5,000 worth of cigarettes and selling them back in six
months for a profit of $15,000; saving enough money
for a trip back to Logar; quitting job as a cashier;
taking wife and three sons back to Logar; walking the
trails and the fields and the orchards of Deh-Naw for
the first time in twenty years; visiting the graves of
Watak and Khoro and the little children of Khoro
and all the other martyrs; telling sons to pray for their
souls, to name their names, to remember.

2001–2007, Lawn Technician, West Sacramento, California

Duties included: moving into a small house in
Broderick only twenty minutes away from youngest
sister at the University of California, Davis; passing
the GED exam; applying for positions of employment
that require a verifiable high school education; driving

a chemical truck to clients' homes in Roseville,
Rocklin, Auburn, Grass Valley, Colusa, Georgetown,
and Stockton, including the house of all-star power
forward Chris Webber; hauling chemicals; spraying
chemicals; breathing chemicals; searching for
pests or decay in grass and gardens and trees;
becoming a top technician by the end of first year;
spraying up to four hundred thousand square feet of
land per year; winning Employee of the Year Award
for 2002; winning Employee of the Year Award for
2003; witnessing the birth of first daughter; training
new recruits; winning Employee of the Year Award
for 2004; working every hour of overtime offered;
waking up at 6:00 in the morning and returning home
at 6:00 in the evening; purchasing a two-story home
in Bridgeway; receiving a top-notch health insurance
plan with dental and eyeglasses; witnessing the birth
of a second daughter; getting passed over for a
promotion in 2005 and 2006 and 2007; getting rear-
ended by a semitruck toward the end of a shift in
2007; tearing nerves in neck and shoulder and spine;
losing the ability to walk for several days; receiving
workers' compensation for exactly one month;
suffering impossible pain in neck and shoulders;
seeing a doctor for the impossible pain in neck and

shoulders and being accused of exaggerating pain;
getting denied further workers' compensation; losing
job; hiring a lawyer.

2007–Infinity, Unemployed, West Sacramento, California

Duties included: filing a suit against former company
for workers' compensation; filing a suit against
trucking company for pain and suffering and medical
bills; applying for disability, Medi-Cal, food stamps,
and welfare; paying court costs and mortgage and
electricity and gas and water and car insurance and
medications out of savings account and maxed-out
credit cards; seeing a second doctor; being prescribed
medication for pain, for migraines, for muscle aches,
for extreme pain, for acid reflux, for blood pressure,
for insomnia, for unbearable pain, for drowsiness, for
dizziness, for constipation, diarrhea, swelling,
stiffness, melancholia; selling gandana and fruit at the
mosque for extra income; allowing wife to sew and
sell Punjabi kali for the first time in her life; accepting
cash from sons after they get part-time jobs in high
school and then college; heading to the emergency
room with oldest son because of pulsing fire in neck
and shoulders; lying on a hospital bed, begging
doctors for help; weeping into burned, calloused,

broken, punctured, hardened, torn, useless hands;
passing out; receiving injections directly into the
spinal cord; settling into a medication and injection
routine that helps to manage the pain; finally winning
the case against trucking company eight years
after the injury; receiving a onetime payment of
$100,000, twenty percent of which goes to the lawyers,
another twenty percent to pay off old debts, and the
rest is injected into the mortgage, hopefully ensuring
that the wife and kids will always have a home;
watching oldest son finish college; attempting to
convince him to pursue law school; gradually
accepting that he plans to study writing; watching
second son finish college with a degree in history (of
all things), learning that he plans to become a teacher;
scraping by month to month on an assortment of
funds ranging from crops to cars to parts to clothes to
lessons in Pashto; falling into terrible, weeklong bouts
of melancholy; attempting to do a bit of yard work
before a sudden movement triggers the lightning bolts
in neck and shoulders; collapsing during tarawih
prayers; applying again for disability with the help of
several doctors of various specialties; standing before a
wealthy white judge who has never labored a day in
his life and hearing that the pain the doctors describe

is not so bad; being rejected for disability; applying
again the next month; hearing word of the death
of the King; returning to Alabama for his funeral;
finding an entire town filled with hundreds of cousins
and nieces and nephews; visiting the family of the
King and leading the janaza prayer; running into the
Captain, who at ninety-something years old is still
filled with rage, though his land in Logar is now
unreachable, though all the old memories are
beginning to become unclear and meaningless, though
oblivion approaches; leaving Alabama until the next
half-brother dies; waiting for sons to begin their
careers; waiting for daughters to begin college; waiting
for wedding days and funerals; waiting for graduations
and good grades; waiting for sleep and food and time
and joy; waiting for the pain to ebb.

A Premonition;
Recollected

Many years later, Mor will think back to her vision of two gunmen, whom she will not remember murdered her brothers, and she will see the gunmen in the night, in the snow, huddled at the base of a mulberry tree, at the end of a pathway, waiting for two orbs of light, orbs like spirits, like twin souls, floating through dark and snow, falling snow, and she will see the cold mist of their breaths, the frost collecting at the tips of the strands of their black beards, and she will see their chapped lips, their gentle eyes watering, and for a moment or two she will wonder why the gunmen in her vision won't go home and huddle in the warmth of an old blanket sewn, perhaps, by a long-forgotten mother, just a girl when she married, a child, kidnapped and beaten and forced into the bedroom of her husband, made to conceive two sons she could never wholly love, before dying in the thousandth bombing of a benevolent American invasion, her boys left behind to be raised by a war that will inevitably lead them to the mouth of an alley in the heart of Logar, and Mor will see their eyes seeing the headlights of her brothers' Corolla tumbling down upon clay and ice and shadow, and she will see the gunmen step out from under the cover of branches into snowfall, into halos of light obscuring the faces of innocent men destined to be martyred for crimes they could never imagine, and she will see the tips of their fingers, already bitten by frost, inch toward the warmth of the trigger.

They must have been so cold, she will think to herself, having forgotten all else.

Waiting for Gulbuddin

*A few years into the war that
is not, for us, a war . . .*

A road in Logar.

A mulberry tree.

Watak's marker, and behind the chinar, a stream.

Me, Gwora, and Mirwais, waiting for Gulbuddin.

Early noon, I turn to Gwora and say: "Let's try it, though, huh?"

"Okay," he says in English, sitting on a dirt mound. "Let

me just . . ." And my little brother yanks at the strap of his torn sandal, trying to get enough pull to retie it. We're speaking English because we're alone, because Malang left us here by Watak's marker (halfway to Mor's house), because Gulbuddin—our second favorite uncle on earth—is supposed to take us the rest of the way.

But he's late, our Gulbuddin, so we wait.

A few feet away, Mirwais, my youngest brother, picks at mulberries on the floor.

"Mirwais," I shout, "don't eat that dirty toot."

Mirwais spits up purple juice. "Smorry," he mumbles.

"Up, up, up, boy," I tell Gwora, who's still sitting on the mound. "Get in position."

"Wait," he says. "I got this."

"Can I get in position?" Mirwais asks. "It's no fun just watching."

"Someone has to watch," I say. "If there's no one to watch—"

"Got it," Gwora yells, and slaps his sandal on the dirt, his toes pulsing purple with blood. He stomps around for a bit, all triumphant, but with every movement his straps strain harder against his skin, until they tear free, and he shouts, "Shit!" too loud, his curse carrying out beyond the trails and the fields, toward the Black Mountains in the distance.

————

"Khar," I say, "you want us to get killed?"

"Who's going to kill us?" Gwora says. "We're kids."

"You see this," I say, and point at the mustache I had been secretly grooming for the past six months. "The marines will think I'm a T."

"The marines won't kill kids," Gwora says.

"Marines love killing kids. You don't remember *Full Metal Jacket*?"

"What do you think is taking Gul so long?" Mirwais interrupts our argument.

"You know how we could kill some time?" I say.

"If we played pretend?" Gwora says.

"If we played pretend," I say.

"What were our roles again?"

"You'll be Watak," I say, "and I'll be the Communist."

⁞

The adhan for Dhuhr rings out over the fields while me and Gwora crouch beneath the mulberry tree—playing pretend. Mirwais sits near Watak's marker and watches us. I've got a stick I'm imagining is a rifle, and I'm searching for Gwora, who is imagining he is unarmed and afraid and sixteen years old. We circle about the mulberry tree like

Elmer Fudd hunting Bugs Bunny. Watak's marker, which is just a red flag tied to a branch held up by a pile of stones, flutters toward the stream behind the chinar. When the adhan is finished, we all turn our heads toward the path from where Gulbuddin is supposed to be coming.

"Should we pray?" Mirwais asks.

"Maybe we should pray," Gwora says.

"Of course we'll pray," I say, "we're not kafir. We'll take a break. We'll pray. But remember where we are."

I kick at the dirt on one side of the tree, and Gwora does the same on the other.

"Don't forget." I point at them both.

We lay our scarves out on the dirt and pray for our families and our friends and for the martyred soul of Watak Shaheed. Back in West Sacramento, a photo of Watak hangs in our prayer room. At only sixteen years old, Watak is our oldest uncle on the earth.

May Allah have mercy on his soul.

"Whose soul?" Mirwais asks.

"Your soul," I say.

"But I'm not dead."

"Not yet."

"I wonder if he's lost," Gwora says, and picks at his straps.

"Gul grew up here," I say. "He won't get lost."

"Watak got lost."

"Watak didn't get lost. He just went down the wrong road."

"What if Gul goes down the wrong road?" Mirwais says.

"He'll be here soon," I say.

"How soon?"

"Just as soon as we finish."

"All right." They sigh and gather their scarves and begin again.

⠿

I hold a branch in my arm like a rifle, but Mirwais doesn't see it.

"Just pretend," I say. "See it like it might be." I point the barrel of the stick at his head. "Are you getting scared?"

"No," he says, and shrugs his shoulders. "Sorry."

A problem: if I can't scare Mirwais, I won't scare anyone.

"What should we do?" I say to Gwora, but he's messing with his straps again.

"Gwora," I say, "just take my sandal."

"I don't want your sandal."

Gwora keeps retying the strap, waits to see if it unties and, when it does, ties it again.

"Marwand," Mirwais says to me, "I need a kamoot."

I point toward the field.

"But it's number two," he says.

"Two," I say. "Dammit, Mirwais, why did you eat all that toot?"

Gwora pulls so hard at the strap of his sandal, he completely tears it off and falls back on the dirt.

"I was hungry," Mirwais says, "I'm still hungry. What if we went back to Agha's house?"

"Ghwul!" Gwora shouts, and tosses his sandal through the chinar.

It plops in the water.

"Give me the stick," Gwora says.

I toss it to him.

Gwora strips his dusmal, wraps it around the stick, and hands it back to me. "Like in *The Godfather*," he says. "Hidden."

I wrap my own dusmal around the stick to give it some more heft and hold it under my armpit and point it at Mirwais's head.

"What about this?" I say.

"It's better," Mirwais says.

"Yeah," I say, looking down its barrel, "it's much better. Now take your shit before we start. No more interruptions!"

Forty-five minutes after he had first left us on the road to wait for Gulbuddin, our cousin-uncle Malang comes strolling back. He has a buddy with him. A scraggly guy with red hair curling out his pakol like a wig. His skin is dark and patchy. Not dark like mud or clay but dark like he'd been up too late too many nights seeing what he shouldn't have seen. And skinny sick. Standing behind Malang, he makes my cousin-uncle's pouch belly stick out even more than it already does. They come up to us, blinking a bunch, with their hands stuffed in their vests.

We stand by the marker.

Mirwais is closest to them.

Then Gwora.

Then me.

"Salaamoona," Malang drawls.

"Walaikum asalaam, Malang Kaka," we say.

"Why is your cousin not"—he scratches his cheek—"in this place . . . yet?"

"He's our uncle," I say.

"He's late," Gwora adds.

Malang furrows his unibrow, takes off his kufi, and

rubs his head. He turns toward his buddy. Though his buddy's lips don't move, Malang nods his head like they've come to an agreement. "We'll be back," he says, and wanders down the road.

⋮

Gwora repeats the second name of God, unarmed, over and over as he stands against the trunk of the mulberry tree. I point my rifle at his chest and say cruel things in what I think is Russian, mocking him and his God.

He looks ready to die.

"No, no, no," I say.

"What?" Gwora says.

"It was pretty good," Mirwais says, tears staining his cheek.

"Something's wrong," I say, and touch the bark of the mulberry tree. It's smooth and unscarred.

"You see Agha's tree?" I tell Gwora. "Chock-full of bullets, deep in the bark."

Gwora slides his fingers along the smooth grooves of Watak's tree. "Oh," he says, "no scars."

"Not one," I say. "It couldn't have been here."

"Then where?" he says.

We all stop and look around. The roads are empty. The

skies are clear (no jets or drones or dragons). The shadows of the chinar grow longer with the dying day. Watak's marker, which is just a flag tied to a branch held up by a pile of stones, flutters in the direction of the stream.

"The water," I say. "He must have fell in the water."

.

Before we can head down toward the stream where Watak died, Malang comes back. This time he has a donkey. Leading it by a rope, he strolls up to us and interrupts our play.

"Malang Kaka," Gwora says, "what happened to your friend?"

Malang smiles. "This is my friend," he says, and pats the donkey on its head.

"That's a donkey," Mirwais says.

"Yes, it is, little nephew, and I need you to watch him for a bit."

He ties the donkey's rope around Watak's mulberry tree, smiles at the chinar trees behind us, and stumbles back down the road.

"Wait," I shout, "what if Gul shows up?"

"Only a minute," he says, and disappears.

Malang's donkey munches on the weeds at the base of

Watak's mulberry tree. Mirwais walks up to it. Pressing down on the donkey's fur with his fingers outstretched, Mirwais whispers: "He's a nice guy." He pets the donkey like it's a Pegasus or a unicorn and stains its hide with mulberry juice. To be honest, it's quite a beautiful donkey. Dark gray hide with a white belly and these big sad eyes that stare right through you. Even when I pick up my rifle and move toward the stream, the donkey's eyes follow me. And when I hop past the chinar and slide down to the bank of the stream, the donkey trots over and watches me from behind the chinar. His eyes follow my every moment, from right to left, up and down, without hardly blinking. "Mirwais," I shout from the bank of the stream, "you're going to be in our play."

"Wallah?" he asks.

"You won't have to watch us anymore," I say, and rush off to make another rifle.

At the bank of the stream between the chinar and the fields, me and Mirwais point our rifles at Gwora—while the donkey watches.

"Where are your brothers," I say, "and what have they stolen and which mujahideen are they helping?"

I speak in what I think is Russian and Mirwais translates everything I say into what he thinks is Pashto. Gwora stands silent in the middle of the stream, looking down into the water. Long shadows of chinar fall on his face and chest. Behind him, the fields rustle softly.

It is almost Asr.

I ask him, again, for the intel, for his brothers, for the wounded mujahideen, but when he refuses to betray his family, I turn toward Mirwais and nod my head, and we raise our rifles. Birds gather in the trees, crickets and lizards scurry among the rocks, even the ants poke out their heads to take a peek. But just as we are about to fire, Gwora looks up from the water, past our rifles, past our heads, and, as if to save himself, points to Watak's flag, which the donkey, at that very moment, is munching. Without really thinking, I swivel on my feet, aim at the eyes of the donkey (he never blinks), and fire six shots in a row.

Blat

Blat

Blat

Blat

Blat

Blat

When the echoes of the shots all die, we trudge up toward
the road.

There, the donkey lies, its hide punctured five times.

Five hits.

Five holes.

Five mouths to close.

Now Mirwais is at its side, and he presses down on the
donkey's wounds, his fingers outstretched, still sticky with
mulberry juice. The blood of the donkey is all over his
hands and his clothes, and he is asking how, and he is asking why, and he is asking you?

I don't respond.

In fact, I hardly move at all before Gwora asks for my
rifle, and I hand it to him, and he breaks the weapon into

many little pieces and tosses them into the stream behind the chinar.

In this way, I think, we both become guilty.

In the red dirt, near the mouth of the donkey, which heaves and shudders and sighs, there is Watak's flag. I pick it up and dust it off, and then, looking toward the highest branches of his mulberry tree, I see the sixth bullet. On its way toward the bark of the branch in which it is now embedded, the bullet pierced a single leaf, and through its puncture, sunlight falls onto the face of the donkey like a halo.

Oh no, I think to myself, our play is over.

The Parable of the Goats

Passed as it was—from mouth to ear to soul, in that small village near the edges of the Black Mountains— word of the humiliating torture, mutilation, murder, and unforgivable desecration of young Saladin's body (who, it was widely known, had spent his entire life hearing the greatly exaggerated tales of his father's jihad against the Soviets, and so, with much trepidation, decided to join up with a small group of melancholic militants, cursed from childhood with the knowledge that they were meant to die violently, at the cusp of manhood, before ever having tasted the bitter nectars of first Love) eventually reached the hairy ears of his giant father, Merzagul. Despite his incredible size, Merzagul was a man with an infamously puny heart, so puny, especially in comparison with the massive width of his chest, that many doctors from various cities all across the nation deemed his breathing life to be a minor medical miracle, something akin to a small tractor engine propelling the flight of a B-52 strategic bomber. And so it was that after Merzagul caught word of the murder of his only son, his puny heart pumped into overdrive and led him to the studded handle of his father's legendary scimitar, which had once chopped down three hundred British colonizers back in the benevolent days of Kipling and Forster, when white men would fight on the earth like mere mortals—not as they did now; from thousands of miles above, from the very heavens themselves, perched upon behemoths of steel and light, watching their targets below, even in the darkest of nights, hour upon hour, spying and recording and listening, until one fateful day or night, when the white men in the clouds would rain down their fire, and decide, with the flick of a finger, the twitch of an eye, the shiver of an asshole, whether an entire village would celebrate a wedding or mourn a funeral.

Still fuming, Merzagul dragged his father's scimitar out onto the road in front of his stolen compound and, in the presence of the entire village, renounced life, love, fatherhood, war, violence, blood, vegetarianism, and, finally, Islam itself, before proceeding to hurl his father's sword into the sky, with the honest intent of murdering Allah (praised is He) Himself.

Then he went back inside to collect his goats.

But by the will of Allah (praised is He), the sword was impeded in its path by an angel.

Twenty-five thousand nine hundred and fifty-eight meters above the spot where Merzagul hurled his father's legendary sword, Second Lieutenant Billy Casteel was flying a McDonnell Douglas F/A-18 twin-engine, supersonic, all-weather, carrier-capable, multirole combat jet, affectionately deemed "the Silver Angel." Casteel had just completed his twentieth bombing mission of the year by successfully obliterating forty-six insurgents, twenty-eight of their young wives, one hundred and fifty-six of their children, forty-eight of their sisters, seventy-three of their younger brothers, nineteen of their mothers, ten of their fathers, twenty-two of their chickens, eight of their cows, three of their bulls, an orchard of their trees, and three thousand honeybees, whose death, it was hypothesized, would eventually lead to the extinction of the human race. The lieutenant was flying back to Home Base, where his closest allies, a small clan of white boys affectionately referred to as "the Rat

Pack" (there was Clinton the Marine and Roger the Navy SEAL and . . .), were waiting to surprise Casteel with a carrot cake and a keg of beer in honor of his twentieth bombing milestone. But as he flew in the sky with the sword of Merzagul's father hurtling toward him, Second Lieutenant Billy Casteel did not feel much like celebrating.

Minutes earlier, as he circled above his targets, Second Lieutenant Billy Casteel made the mistake of peering down and glancing upon a flock of baby goats led by two tiny shepherds who couldn't have been more than six years old. Briefly, Second Lieutenant Billy Casteel was reminded of his own childhood on a goat farm in Davis, California, where he once cared for his father's flock alongside his older brother, David, who died one night falling off a horse on a ride through the dark woods near their farm, a ride Casteel had suggested despite the darkness and the cold and his brother's frail heart. In the years after his brother's death, Billy had abandoned his father's goats and taken refuge in computer-generated pornography, online social simulations, catfish accounts on Instagram, the philosophy of Jean Baudrillard, the writings of Philip K. Dick, and the *Modern Warfare* franchise, through which he had carried out his first virtual drone strike on little blips of Afghan enemies. Well, those boys could be me and Davey, Second Lieutenant Billy Casteel thought to himself before his desensitization training kicked in and he turned the blips on his screen into blossoms of light. Eventually, though, Casteel was struck by what he thought was a terrible pang of guilt.

In reality, it was the sword.

Tumbling from the heavens, Second Lieutenant Billy Casteel managed to spread his arms and legs as if he were prepared to embrace the earth itself, creating enough drag to deploy his parachute and float softly toward an inconspicuous little village he had yet to bomb. He landed in the branches of a mulberry tree, one of which, as if instructed by Allah (praised is He) Himself, promptly struck Casteel in the head, knocking him out.

⁝

Bubugul was on her way to Hajji Alo's mosque for the Dhuhr prayer when she spotted a soldier hanging from Watak's mulberry tree, just high enough to seriously hurt himself, and although her daily prayers were the only true comfort in her life, Bubugul decided it would please her Lord to sacrifice her salah and help him down. At one hundred and twenty-three years old, Bubugul had secretly hoped to die for over half a century, and it would have broken her heart to know that Azrael, the angel of death, had visited the Earth over fifty-three years ago to take her life, but Bubugul had such a knack for preserving the sanctity of life, wherever she found it, human or beast, plant or insect, fungi or bacteria, that the Earth itself could not bear to let her go. On several occasions, Azrael had flown to the Earth so as to inquire about the life of Bubugul, and every time the Earth had found some excuse to keep her alive.

"One hundred and twenty-two years," Azrael had recounted earlier that same year.

"Azrael," the Earth replied, "I have sacrificed my youth, my beauty, my health, and perhaps my very life, all for the sake of Allah's (praised is He) creation, and yet, every year, only He knows why, Allah sends fewer companions to look after me in the autumn of my life."

The Earth had a point.

Out of all of the billions of planets in the vast universe, only the Earth had been selected to accept the burden of hosting humanity. Once last year, Azrael had lied to himself, before he flew back to Home Base, empty-handed.

Bubugul collected a bundle of leaves beneath the feet of

the soldier and went off to locate a military translator in the next village just as Merzagul—who happened to be leading his beloved herd of goats toward the Black Mountains in search of his son's corpse—came upon Casteel. With his giant fingers trembling, Merzagul yanked Casteel from the tree like an unripe mulberry and tossed him over his shoulder. Followed closely by his goats, who leapt at Merzagul's back, attempting to nip at the yellow hair of the soldier he carried, Merzagul journeyed back home, announcing along the way that the entire village was invited to his compound for a feast.

●
○

Merzagul and his wife, Talwasa, had always been known as formidable cooks, but it was only after the arrival of his mountain goats that Merzagul's reputation as a chef superseded the legend of his rage. The story went that a few nights after his youngest and most beloved daughter was married off to a well-to-do Pashtun from the city, Merzagul fell into a terrible depression. His once-crowded compound had been emptied by the suitors who had come, one after the other, to marry his seven daughters. The first proposition had elated him. The boy was good and clean and strong, from a well-known family just two towns over, and he held a reliable position as a teacher. The second daughter was married off shortly afterward, then the third, and it was only after the wedding of his fourth daughter that the suitors began to annoy him. When he declared that none of his remaining daughters would be wed for the next three years, the suitors seemed to become even more brazen. They came from as far as Paktia and Jalalabad, bearing magnificent gifts and impressive reputations, until, eventually, Merzagul's conscience would not allow him to deny his daughters such pleasant lives. And so, after he gave his youngest daughter to the boy from the city, Merzagul became inconsolable and refused to eat. For three days and three nights, Merzagul fasted, denying himself his favorite dishes (chapli, seekh, and shami kebabs, landi, kofta, roasted lamb, and goat's intestine), until the morning of the fourth day, when he awoke to find his courtyard packed with baby goats from the Black Mountains. The night before, American forces had firebombed the Black Mountains, and the goats there, barely escaping the carnage, had ventured down to the valley and taken shelter in Merzagul's home. Without a hint of guilt, Merzagul proceeded to pick up each of the goats and toss them out onto the roads. But no matter how far or how frequently he threw the goats, they always managed to find their way back into his courtyard. Eventually, he gave up on his battle and returned to his hunger and silence. The goats, on the other hand, would not go hungry so quietly. All day and all night, for two days and two nights straight, the goats wept loudly for sustenance. To placate them, Talwasa made every attempt short of cutting their throats, but something about the traumas they'd suffered from the war had made them uneasy. Then, on the seventh morning of his starvation, Merzagul could not put up with their incessant moaning any longer. He went out into his courtyard with the largest butcher knife he owned. There, seeing the weeping goats, so dark and lost and scared, Merzagul found that his puny heart had overcome his mammoth rage. Still determined to quiet their weeping, he took up his wife's mission to feed them. That was why, one afternoon, Talwasa happened to walk in on her husband as he knelt on all fours and began to nibble at a pile of hay. In the beginning, he only pretended to eat, but when the hay touched his starving tongue, its scent of life overwhelmed him. He ate with relish. The goats joined him in his feast. From then on, Merzagul and his beloved goats shared every meal together. His newfound vegetarian diet seemed to restore in him a lost vigor. Nine months later, his wife gave birth to their first and only son, Saladin.

•
◦

Fortunately for his guests, Merzagul's vegetarianism had done nothing to dilute the quality of his dishes, and, in fact, had only enhanced his wizardry in the kitchen. He prepared their entire meal on his own, chopping wood and lighting fires and sweating away in the tandoor khana while running back and forth between several different pots of stews in the courtyard. He was cooking all twenty-four of Saladin's favorite dishes at once. His wife, Talwasa, had locked herself up in Saladin's old bedroom and taken to smelling his old clothes before the memory of his musk faded from the world. Near Asr, Merzagul's guests came with their own dishes, figuring that the couple couldn't possibly cook for their entire village, and yet before them lay such an assortment of marvelous platters that even the lingering scent of Merzagul's sweat, which had been kneaded into the dough and dripped into the stews, could not spoil their appetite. Merzagul's mountain goats ate the same food tossed in a small trough near the orchard, where everyone supposed Merzagul was hiding his American.

Past the doorway into the orchard, past the apple trees and the garden, past the flower bushes and the swing he'd built sixteen years ago for his only son, Merzagul had dug a pit. It was two meters wide and three meters deep and it was covered with a makeshift barricade Merzagul had fashioned from striplings and chinar. Inside this pit, near the farthest corner of the orchard, Second Lieutenant Billy Casteel sat up against a mud wall, wearing nothing but his underwear. Merzagul and his guests crowded the pit, some of them inching toward its edges while others climbed up into the surrounding trees and hung from the branches. Faithful in the strength of his cage, Merzagul made no attempt to push anyone back, and when he saw that every single one of his guests had entered the orchard and seen the soldier, he finally offered his proposition.

"On this day," he declared to his neighbors and friends and even a few enemies, "I offer you all your God-given right to mortal justice. Beginning tomorrow morning, immediately after the Fajr salah, every single one of you, from the eldest woman to the youngest boy, will be given a turn with the soldier. You may use your turn as you wish, except that there will be no psychological tortures and no dark magic. Understood?"

Some of his guests readily agreed and some declined to

be involved, but no one was prepared to deny anyone else their turn with the soldier. The long war had mutilated many families and bodies and souls, and its perpetrators had remained invisible for so long that it almost seemed as if it had become a natural phenomenon, like an eternal tornado, but now here it was, the war itself, captured in the body of a little yellow-headed man in his dirty underwear.

•

The next morning, just after the Fajr salah, every single one of Merzagul's guests returned to his orchard, either to witness or to take part in the punishment of the soldier. Some carried clubs and stones, knives and cleavers, some had irons and hammers and pots filled with boiling oil or tar or just water. Some brought Tasers and peppers and lemon juice. Cleverly, it seemed to some, Merzagul had actually given the soldier his first punishment by refusing to feed him. Second Lieutenant Billy Casteel hadn't eaten since the day before, and some believed that the succulent scents of the feast were, in and of themselves, a form of torture. Unfortunately, it didn't have its desired effect. Second Lieutenant Billy Casteel sat in the middle of the pit, legs crossed, calmly building an alien city out of mud while chanting a Gothic tune from an old first-person shooter he once loved. Apparently, the night had been cold, for the soldier had rubbed himself, head to toe, in mud. He sat there in the pit, chanting and humming and carving sepulchres for an ancient warrior class of genocidal aliens, and did not even look up to acknowledge his captors. Naturally, Merzagul's guests began to fashion a line based on seniority, but before anyone else could take their turn, Bubugul the Saint entered the orchard. Taking small, measured steps so as not to crush any stray spiders or wandering insects, she approached the edge of the pit where Casteel lay.

The crowd parted for Merzagul.

"You're punishing this soldier?" Bubugul asked, peering down at the dirty creature playing in the mud.

"We're *all* punishing this soldier," Merzagul replied.

"Would you mind, then?"

"Mind what, Bibi?"

"If I took part."

"Of course not," Merzagul said. "You are our mother."

The crowd murmured in agreement. Bubugul was much loved and much feared because none of the villagers could recall a time before their love and their fear of Bubugul.

Her eternal presence in the village and her seeming proximity to the otherworld gave her an almost spectral quality, like a benevolent ghost that had always haunted them and always would.

"Allow me fifteen minutes," Bubugul said, and exactly fourteen minutes later, she reentered the orchard, leading along a young and handsome mountain goat, which, with Merzagul's permission, gracefully climbed down into the hole with the soldier.

"I'm very sorry," Bubugul muttered, though no one was certain if she was speaking to the soldier or the crowd or the goat.

Initially, the second lieutenant's plan had been to murder, eat, and then wear the goat's skin for warmth. He had slaughtered hundreds of goats on his family's farm in Davis and was already visualizing how he might use his teeth to tear open the skin on the creature's neck. Momentarily, though, he was outarmed. The large and handsome mountain goat had two spiraling horns like corkscrews and impossibly spry limbs, while the lieutenant's strength had been sapped from him by hunger. He was not sure if he could charge and pin and suffocate the goat head-on.

If he wanted to survive, he had to be clever. Overnight, a few apples from the orchard had fallen into his pit, and though he was famished, his soldier's intuition had told him to bury the fruit and wait. "Billy," he said to the goat sitting before him, and held out an apple in the splintered sunlight. Gingerly, the goat trotted forward, its head cocked, it eyes empty. The second lieutenant placed the apple on the roof of a miniature mud tower he had constructed to pass the time and stepped back within an arm's reach of the bait. The goat cocked its head in the opposite direction, its eyeballs trembling, and leaned forward. Within an inch of the apple, just as the second lieutenant was reaching for its neck, the goat turned its face and chomped down on his extended hand with such force, it took the second lieutenant a few seconds to realize he was wounded. Bleeding profusely, he passed out.

Hours later, the second lieutenant awoke to the Isha adhan in a darkness so thick he could not tell if the goat was still near him. Its scent seemed to linger. He thought he could hear the huffing of its breath, the clopping of its hooves. His hand no longer bled, but when he felt for the wound in the dark, he realized that it had been plugged up with something resembling hair or fur. He was too afraid to tear it away. After shuffling toward the edge of the pit, the soldier sat up against a wall and attempted to recall his survival training. He needed to build up his psychological defenses. He needed to remain wary. But all through the night, the huffing, clopping, chomping, pissing, shitting, twisting, climbing, farting, spitting, and whispering of the mountain goat would not allow him to focus. With time, again, he passed out.

In the morning, there were two goats.

Wholly identical, both goats sat on the farthest edge of the pit and seemed to stare into each of the soldier's eyes. It was as if the goat had replicated itself in the night, or as if the one goat had been split into two. He attempted to avoid their gaze for as long as he could, but he found that there were ways to become lost in the face of a goat. There was something comforting in the creases, the horns, the teeth, the beard. The oddly human eyes. Touching his makeshift bandage, he noticed that there was more fur sprouting from his wound. When night fell, the soldier thought he heard chatter coming from the other side of the pit. At first, he was sure that his captors were playing tricks on him, that this was all a part of the torture, the breakdown, but as the night wore on, the voices quieted, and he fell asleep touching the hairs of his wound.

In the morning, there were four goats.

All of them, again, identical.

Like this, day after day, the goats replicated themselves, splitting from two to four to eight to sixteen, as the fur or the hair spread from the base of his wound to his fingers and wrist. Eventually, the pit was stuffed with so many goats that he felt them against his skin at all times. He listened to their tongues and smelled their scents, which, he realized, was his scent too. No longer afraid, he nestled himself into a spot near the center of the pit. He could not recall his survival tactics, the basics of his military training, the names of his commanding officers, or the early years of his youth when the scent of goats had awakened him every morning. He had loved a boy with a frail heart, he had attempted to drown himself in a shallow creek, he had masturbated to horrifying scenes of violence, he had obliterated many blips on many screens, he had had a name and a rank and a calling, but he had forgotten, and as he kept on forgetting, the chatter of the goats became more sensible.

The goats complained of the size of the pit and began a digging operation to increase the area of their abode. In the beginning, the man refused to assist his neighbors. He

nestled into his spot, nursing his wounds and his memories, weeping without shame as the goats made the most of
their situation. They dug and built tunnels and fashioned
individual pits within the pit so that each coupling of goats
could have their own space and privacy. They even built
the man his own personal pit within the pit, and this act of
kindness affected him so deeply, he began to take part in
their labors. Crawling on all fours, he dug with the goats
and listened to their songs and stories and poems and jokes.
He clawed at mud with his elbows and knees. He swallowed mouthfuls of dirt and shat pebbles in his wake. He
rubbed his forehead against hard, dark clay and felt it
chasm into a home. He bleated.

.
.

By way of one peculiar goat's insistence on making up for
its lost labors, the herd discovered within their tunnels an
underground cavern filled with clear mountain water and
stones covered in moss. The goats drank from this water
and licked these stones, and like this, for a time, they persisted through the tunnels, past the cavern, into the upper
hollows, where they found ancient halls filled with gold

and diamonds and priceless artifacts. Ignoring these trea-
sures, the goats trotted toward the outer regions of the caves
and escaped out onto the tops of the Black Mountains.
From the heights of the cliffs, the goats traveled down onto
the valley and entered a small village and arrived at the
door of a compound they vaguely remembered. One of
these goats—distinguished by its golden fur—knocked on
the large door with the tip of its newly sprouted horn.
Therein, they were met by a giant, and this giant, seeing for
the second time in his life a mysterious herd of mountain
goats escaped from the Black Mountains, proceeded to invite them inside and vowed to treat them with love and
care until the day of his death, which came shortly afterward, when a rogue squadron of commandos—known as
"the Rat Pack"—broke into his compound, slaughtered him
and his wife and every single one of his goats in a mad operation attempting to locate a missing and beloved pilot who
once went by the name Second Lieutenant Billy Casteel.

.
.

Upon arriving in the village for the souls of the dead, Azrael
visited Bubugul and found her shuddering inconsolably on

a thin toshak. She begged for death and wept until she fell asleep. Overcome with mercy, the angel of death then entered her dreams and sat by her side and told her so many stories of life that she became utterly convinced she had died.

The Tale of
Dully's Reversion

1

Shakako Jani was praying Fajr beneath the makeshift shrine she had built for her two martyred brothers, Fahim and Kadeem, when, at approximately six forty-five a.m., Dully Abdul Kareem, her second-born son, crossed the path of her janamaz and promptly transformed into a small monkey. And although, as she would later recall, Shakako did not see the transformation—her eyes being fixed upon her janamaz—she did hear the cracking sound of seven English rifles being fired from somewhere deep within the Black Mountains, and because she knew that the Black

Mountains were eight thousand miles away, in Logar, and that the last of the English rifles in Naw'e Kaleh were sold for a hundred pieces of cornbread in 1982, during the worst months of the massacre-famines, she realized that the cracking sound she heard was not of death but of a different sort of reversion. Thus, upon finishing her prayer, Shakako knelt forward, picked through her son's fallen leather satchel, his striped cardigan, and his unlocked cell phone (the first draft of an email lingering on its screen), to find Dully sleeping atop seven perfectly round pellets of his own shit. She lifted her son into her arms and rushed to call the Imam.

"He's on the run," the Imam's second and most honest wife, Gulapa, informed Shakako over the phone. Purportedly, a local squadron of Ts intended to execute the Imam for an old war crime he had not carried out during the initial stages of the American invasion in 2001. Gulapa went on to promise Shakako that the Imam had promised her that a different squadron of Ts had promised him that the whole situation would blow over before the Isha salah.

"Inshallah," Shakako said, and hung up her phone with a slight click, awakening Dully.

•
•

Moments before his transformation, Dully was frantically completing an email to a student who had incorrectly addressed him as Dr. Maslan, whose name was listed on the registry for the class, though Professor Michèle Maslan hadn't taught an introductory course since the 1990s. Because Dully had forgotten to correct her in his initial response, he felt it too late to fix the mistake in his subsequent emails and so had been ending his letters with Maslan's signature phrase: "Verily yours, Dr. Maslan." The student had suggested that Dully might have assigned too many texts. What the student didn't know was that Dully had *especially* assigned too many texts for an Introduction to Islam course he was not qualified to teach, and yet he still needed to *introduce* Islam and felt an overwhelming pressure to explicate every political, theological, philosophical, and historical nuance of a fourteen-hundred-year-old religion he was no longer sure belonged to him. His students were upset— they could hardly contain their passive aggression in their emails—and he knew that the only reason he had not been reported to the department for the absurd amount of reading assignments was that all of his students had assumed he was the legendary and fearful Dr. Maslan, who was so old and tenured and French, she probably could have water-boarded her students in class without it much affecting her teaching career.

To go along with his ongoing impersonation of Dr. Maslan, Dully was also busy deceiving his thesis adviser, Professor Rabbani. A distant relative and an outspoken critic of the former president of Afghanistan, Burhanuddin Rab-bani, Professor Rabbani (the American) had achieved a sort of mythic status after having almost been assassinated in Kabul by rabid devotees of the dead warlord Ahmad Shah Massoud. He now lived in exile in San Francisco. When Dully had first walked into Professor Rabbani's office three years earlier, he had hoped that their shared nationality and abhorrence of warlords would create a bond of friend-ship and mutual respect. Dully was seeking an adviser, a mentor. Rabbani, unfortunately, had been seeking a servant. He immediately tasked Dully with combing through end-less archives of Soviet-era Afghan propaganda for cartoon depictions of both Communist and mujahideen factions for *his* next book on the signification of the "warlord" in con-temporary Afghan history. Dully resisted subjugation the only way he knew how: anxiety-inducing procrastination.

He was approximately four months behind on his assignment but had been able to keep Rabbani at bay with a series of increasingly complex lies, assuring his adviser that his nonexistent contacts in Kabul had come upon a treasure chest of never-before-seen propagandist material, which was, unfortunately, caught up in Kabul's infamous bureaucratic red tape. Dully had gone on to actually convince his adviser that he was planning to visit Kabul University within the next few weeks to resolve the issue in person. And though Dully knew that both of his ruses had gone on for far too long, he still continued to find himself replying to students in the guise of Maslan mere hours before his first class, which also happened to be around the same time that he carelessly stepped in front of his mother's janamaz and transformed into a small monkey.

Through the cascading sunlight of a cramped kitchen in West Sacramento, California, Dully blinked his tender eyeballs and peered up at the single strand of hair stubbornly jutting out of his mother's otherwise hairless chin. For many years, Dully's mother had refused to pluck this particular strand of hair, considering it holy, a gift from God, from which little angels surely swung. And until very recently, when the labors of scholarly worship had zapped all physical vanity from Dully's sense of himself (or so it seemed), he had been deeply embarrassed by what he secretly referred to as his mother's "goatee." The children at his elementary school used to mock his mother's appearance in English—knowing that she didn't understand—and Dully still felt ashamed that he had never defended her, even once.

Seeing her son's eyes water in the morning light, Shakako instinctively shielded his face with her chador, the tips of which she had forgotten were coated in cumin, causing Dully to sneeze with such a fury, he fell to the kitchen floor.

Fortunately, Dully landed on his feet.

Standing up at full length, Dully bared his fangs and lifted his arms and legs, one at a time, as if to test them. Morning light fell upon him in slats, brightening his already luminous blond fur. His heart thumped in his chest at such a rapid pace, he could feel the blood racing from its ventricles into his veins, each and every vein, which initially had been terrifying, but, quickly adjusting to its pace and force, he began to feel, oddly enough, healthy.

Exponentially healthy. Or, that is to say, healthier than he had felt in years. In fact, ever since the day he started his PhD in the History of Revolution program at UC Sacramento, Dully had become so fully immersed in the life of the mind—in reading, writing, research, analysis, argumentation, references, notes, subnotes, emails, translations, firsthand accounts, secondhand accounts, email threads, faculty gossip, and so on and so forth—that for large swaths of time, his body ceased to matter to him. His hair had been falling out. He had been losing weight and muscle and dexterity. His bones hurt all the time for no reason. He had become sallow and gaunt and could fit into only the slimmest and most stylish of clothing. But now, in his monkey's body, with his heart pumping wildly in his chest, he seemed calm, almost content.

That was, until he spoke.

"Where is my phone?" Dully said, or thought he said, because all that came out of his mouth was an odd warbling sound. "I've got class," he went on warbling. "I must teach. I must . . ." Horrified by his sudden inability to speak English with the eloquence he had so tirelessly developed over the course of grade school, middle school, high school, college, and the first three years of his PhD program, Dully shrieked, heard his own shrieking, frightened himself, and scurried off into the living room, where his grandmother Bibi Halima and his father, Gran Ghorzang, sat on separate beige couches, arguing in Pashto and Farsi about whether to watch TOLO or Lemar for the latest updates on the clashes in Logar. Gunfights between the Ts and the government militias were supposed to have been intensifying, and both Bibi and Gran wished to see how close the fighting was to their old village. But in the midst of their ongoing argument, they stopped to watch a small, beautiful monkey leap onto their coffee table and begin to shriek with what sounded like a deeply philosophical desperation. Almost in unison, Gran and Bibi cocked back the personal remotes each of them safeguarded like a favorite sword, but before they had a chance to strike the monkey down, Shakako burst in, shouted three variations of the second name of Allah, and declared that the monkey before them was not just a monkey but her son.

First, Bibi asked: "Did he cross the path of your janamaz?"

Second, Gran added: "Did you call the Imam?"

"Yes," Shakako said to them both, slightly wheezing.

"You're always praying too late," Bibi scolded Shakako in Farsi, and went on to prophesize that Shakako's habit of praying late, and Dully's transformation into a monkey, was just another sign of the fast-approaching Day of Judgment.

"What did the Imam say?" Gran asked in Pashto.

"According to his wife, Qadir is on the run."

"Which wife?"

"The second one."

"That's the honest one."

"I hope so."

"When is he supposed to return?"

"A few hours. She promised."

"Then it'll be a day or two," Gran said. "At least."

⁞

A few hours later, the home phone rang exactly twice before Gran picked up.

"It's me," the Imam's voice sounded from the speaker, and cut off.

Gran returned Qadir's call using one of the burners he purchased at different shops on different days of the week at least once a month to outwit the federal agents who had been stalking him since the day a wealthy Saudi dissident successfully arranged for the destruction of two buildings

Gran had only ever seen in a particularly amusing episode of *The Simpsons*.

"Imam Sahib," Gran hollered into his burner, "I heard the big beards were after you?"

Though there was a certain animosity between Gran and Imam Qadir—during the Soviet war they had fought for rival mujahideen factions and both, at different times, had vied for the hand of Shakako—Gran still respected the Imam's propensity for miracles. According to Logari lore, over the course of the Soviet invasion, the mujahideen civil wars, and the American occupation, Imam Qadir had been shot, mutilated, hung, choked, electrocuted, struck with shrapnel, blown up, starved, poisoned, drowned, and shot again but would not die because his body was propelled by the spirit of the Quran, whose message he would keep on delivering from village to village until the Day of Judgment.

"Alhamdulillah," the Imam replied. "It was merely a case of mistaken identity. The boys were searching for an old mujahid named Imam Qabir and came after me by mistake. Can you blame them? Only a letter off, you know, but once they heard who I was, they apologized, may Allah protect them. Sweet boys, you know, not unlike your son. How is he?"

"Akmal is well. He is studying Quran in Egypt. He has a son now."

"Mashallah! I forgot you had become a grandfather. And what about Abdullah?"

Dully sat on the farthest edge of Bibi's beige couch, typing away at his phone with both hands like a tablet. Upon being groomed and clothed by his mother, Dully had immediately fallen back into his old habit of interacting with nothing and no one save for his laptop and cell phone. With the sleeves of his toddler's kameez rolled up to the elbow, Dully edited the second draft of an email to Dr. Maslan, who determined teaching appointments every year. According to the tenth years in his PhD program, Maslan's teaching reviews were particularly brutal and uncompromising on account of the fact that her secretly utilitarian objective was to weed out weaklings from her program so as to slightly improve the abysmal academic job market. Number one on her list of infractions was not showing up to teach.

Dear Dr. Maslan, his email began. *I seem to have come down with some sort of . . .*

"And how exactly did the miracle occur?" the Imam asked Gran, who turned to Shakako, who related her account of Dully's transformation, pausing every few seconds to give Gran enough time to repeat the story back to the Imam, until near the very end, when the Imam interrupted Gran's recounting of Shakako's story in order to ask how often Dully prayed.

Using his phone's text-to-speech app, Dully told his mother, who told her husband, who told the Imam that he hadn't sincerely prayed a salah in a very long time.

"How long?" the Imam asked.

Two years, four months, twelve days, and seven hours. The last prayer Dully had faithfully prayed was the Isha salah on the twenty-seventh night of Ramadan. Immediately upon completing his prayer, Dully had begun to read the Human Rights Watch report *Blood-Stained Hands: Past Atrocities in Kabul and Afghanistan's Legacy of Impunity,* where he came upon the following passages: *A Junbish official detailed some of the specific commanders involved in abuses: Shir Arab, Ismail Diwaneh ["Ismail the Mad"], and Abdul Cherik [109] from the beginning engaged in widespread looting of the market. Killing took place only over looting. In late 1371, early 1372 [January to May 1993], they looted the Porzeforooshi Bazaar. . . . Ismail Diwaneh was in Bala Hissar [on the southeast edge of Kabul]. He regularly killed and robbed Pashtuns from Paktia who were passing through on the way to Kabul.[110] Another former Shura-e Nazar official, discussing general looting by Jamiat forces in 1992 and 1993, described a particularly bad commander, Rahim "Kung Fu," who the official said was "a robber and killer and a thief, in a word, a criminal."[111] The official (who began crying as he was interviewed about Rahim) also told Human Rights Watch that Rahim was involved in killings of Hazara civilians, and children, during an operation against Wahdat forces posted in Taimani neighborhood in 1992: "There were many rapes, the killing of many women and men. He was killing so many Hazaras. He killed children. I'm sorry, I cannot talk about it anymore."[112] In a later interview, he described how he heard Rahim boast about crimes committed during the Taimani operation: He said he* pochaghed *[slaughtered, or cut their throats] Hazara. "We killed 300, 350 people," he said. "I went to a house. I saw an infant. I put the bayonet in its mouth. It sucked on it like a tit, then I pushed it through."[113]* This led Dully to read further accounts on the specific methods of torture used throughout the Soviet occupation, the Afghan civil wars, and the US occupation, which led him into a wormhole of internet searches and documents and videos until he found himself on a shady Russian forum with videos of

Syrians being tortured by Assad's forces in a manner eerily similar to the techniques used by KHAD in Afghanistan. He watched bones being crushed by sledgehammers. He watched children being burned alive with torches. He watched grainy, close-up shots of castrations. He watched clip after clip of systematic rape and mutilation and murder, and all the while, he kept justifying that to take witness, to record and analyze atrocities, was his duty as a scholar, as a historian, as a . . . But the clips, the photographs, even the textual descriptions, warped something in his understanding of his own body. Often, he stared at his hands, touched his skin, and attempted to make sense of all the atrocities that could be committed against flesh, and this contemplation left him sleepless and depressed and afraid. He wondered why God had made humans so malleable, so soft, only to be torn apart on highways or systematically mutilated in dark chambers and black sites, at the hands of beloved men, until the mind could no longer comprehend the suffering of the body and destroyed itself.

That was when Dully stopped praying.

"Then the problem seems clear to me," the Imam said. "Abdullah has allowed kufr to infect his heart, to spread throughout his veins and muscles and the very strands of his

DNA, until it physically manifested itself when he egregiously crossed his mother's janamaz. This is what I recommend: Abdullah must flee the land of kufr, at once, and he must come to me here in Logar. Then, together, we will visit the shrine of Hajji Hotak in the Black Mountains, and if he is able to fast for three days and three nights in the darkness of the shrine, his fear and his hunger may replenish his faith in Allah and return his body to a state of fitrah—inshallah."

"Inshallah," Gran repeated as if he agreed, but after he hung up the phone, he turned to his family and said: "Well, Qadir has lost his mind. But I suppose you can only be killed so many times before you begin suggesting visits to the shrine of Hajji Hotak."

"Hajji Hotak was a martyr of the highest caliber," Bibi declared.

"Hajji Hotak was a coward and a pimp," Gran replied. "He had five wives and twenty-seven children, all of whom he left to die when he tried to flee Naw'e Kaleh during the English massacres. His shrine won't be any more holy than Najibullah's grave."

"Which massacre is this?" Dully asked with his phone, abandoning his email to Maslan.

"The winter massacres of 1315," Gran answered.

Searching Google, Dully converted 1315 AH to AD 1897. "But there was no war in 1897. Why would the English have been committing a massacre in Logar then?" Dully asked, but the soft, computerized voice of his phone was overtaken by Bibi.

"Hajji Hotak," Bibi said, "didn't have a wife or a child to his name. He was an old cripple, half-mad, and *he* was abandoned by his family, because he slowed them down in the mountains. Hotak was the first Logari to die in the massacres."

"And how did Hotak die?" Shakako asked.

"By firing squad," Gran answered.

"I heard seven rifles being fired from the Black Mountains the exact moment that Dully transformed," Shakako said.

"You see," Bibi shouted. "Do you see now? It is a sign!"

Gran didn't see. He shut his eyes to stave off a migraine and quietly declared to his family that no one was going to Logar, or anywhere else, without him or his permission. Then he rose up out of his seat, careful not to trigger the eternal nerve damage in his neck and shoulders, and retired to the dark of his bedroom.

"What an actress," Bibi muttered as soon as her son was gone. Bibi tsk-tsked and Dully tap-tapped and Shakako fell into pondering the echoes of English rifles until she heard the voices of her two young daughters, Shirin and Shama, reverberate from the hall.

Quickly, she tossed a shawl onto Dully.

Ten and twelve, respectively, Shirin and Shama had waited for the fighting to die before crossing the living room into the kitchen.

"Wah," Bibi shouted, "no salaam?"

"No time for salaams," Shirin joked, and began preparing an abominable vegetable smoothie in accordance with an Olympian figure skater's diet she had read about on a Tumblr blog. The girls diced and cooked and blended, and Shakako watched her daughters rush about her kitchen from the living room as if the girls were being projected onto a film screen, and she felt a hopeless urge to utter many sweet nothings at them, none of which she actually uttered, until after the girls had already departed with their book bags and hijabs, leaving Shakako to deal with the problem of her son.

•
•

Sitting beneath the shrine for her two martyred brothers, Fahim and Kadeem, Shakako recited the Quran and occasionally blew duas in her son's direction. Dully crouched a few feet away, encircled by a short wall of textbooks and memoirs and other historical accounts. Though there were twenty unread emails in his in-box from students and advisers and there was a deadline coming up for his grant proposal and there was the research he still owed Professor Rabbani and there were stacks of reading responses he had yet to grade for the Intro to Islam course he was forced to teach, Dully scoured his books for some hint of a clue of a previously unrecorded English massacre in Logar, which could significantly expand the breadth (and depth) of his dissertation project, tentatively titled "Historical Erasure and State Violence in the Logar Province of Afghanistan."

Shakako stopped reciting.

Her ninety-nine duas had done nothing to alter her son's condition, and with the realization that she almost certainly could not pray Dully to salvation, a disturbing thought flourished in her mind, and this thought, having flourished, fed into other thoughts and ideas, until a series of ideas had turned into an absurd plan she could not help but utter. . . . "Dully," Shakako said, "what if we left?"

Dully looked up from his books for the first time in hours.

Above his mother's head, the framed photographs of Fahim and Kadeem were polished and perfumed and garlanded with lilies.

Then, all at once, the perfect email came to him:

Dear Professor,

I am escorting my mother to Afghanistan for the funeral services of her two younger brothers. They have been murdered. I hope to be back within a few weeks. In the meantime, it may be difficult to reach me.

Best Regards,
Abdul
PhD Candidate
The History of Revolution
University of California, Sacramento

2

Neither Shakako nor Dully slept much at all during their flight. To go along with the insistent pain in her knees, Shakako was tormented by the guilt of having "stolen" her own wedding gold—which she had hoped to gift to Shirin and Shama on their respective wedding days—in order to pay for their tickets at the Reno-Tahoe International Airport. The arms of her impossibly small chair dug into her sides, and her feet had swollen up, but because the German passenger sitting one aisle over kept leering in her direction, she didn't dare remove her slippers. Shakako was a tall, handsome woman, and though she wore hijab for the sake of her haya, she knew it often drew more attention than it diverted. How shameful of the Turks, she thought, with their fancy airline and their halal meals and their Islamist president and yet without the common courtesy to provide a believing woman with the option to separate herself from the eyes of perverted men.

Several feet below Shakako, Dully sat comfortably inside of an extra-large pet carrier, in the cargo hold of the plane, reading Winston Churchill's field reports from the Mohmand campaign of 1897–1898 by the dim light of his cell phone: *On the morning of the 16th,* it began, *in pursuance of Sir Bindon Blood's orders, Brigadier-General Jeffreys moved out of his entrenched camp at Inayat Kila, and entered the Mamund Valley. His intentions were, to chastise the tribesmen by burning and blowing up all defensible villages within reach of the troops. . . . Firing began on the left at about nine o'clock, and a quarter of an hour later the guns came into action near the centre. The Guides and Buffs now climbed the ridges to the right and left. The enemy fell back according to their custom, "sniping." Then the 38th pushed forward and occupied the village, which was handed over to the sappers to destroy. This they did most thoroughly, and at eleven o'clock a dense white smoke was rising from the houses and the stacks of bhoosa. . . . The enemy's losses were considerable, but no reliable details could be obtained. . . .*

Though it was officially recorded that Churchill's Malakand Field Force went only as far north as Koda Khel in Khyber Pakhtunkhwa, burning villages all along the way, Dully hoped to find some brief reference to a rogue regiment or an instance of imperial justice gone too far north, into the valleys and villages of the sovereign nation of Afghanistan, where, perhaps, a particularly ambitious general started slaughtering Pashtun tribesmen beyond the borders of the Durand Line. Certainly, it was a long shot, but Dully's parents' stories of forgotten massacres had served him well in the past. They were, in fact, the very crux of his stalled dissertation project. In recent months, Dully had fallen so far behind with his own research, the prospect of finishing his dissertation within the decade seemed almost impossible. That was, until he found himself in the

---

cargo hold of an airplane on its way to Kabul, reading and writing and pondering upon historical massacres with such glee, he briefly worried for the state of his soul.

On the morning Gran discovered that his wife had fled to Logar without him or his permission, he felt such a momentous rage stir in his heart that even when it triggered the lightning bolts in his neck and shoulders, he kept cursing and shouting and fueling his anger, until the bolts were popping off at such a consistent rate, and with such a terribly aching fury, that Gran was able to reach the nexus of the pain of his wound, within which, he had always feared, lay the abyss. But rather than death, he discovered a whole new plane of existence whereby his aching both fueled and negated his rage. And vice versa. Therefore, using the momentum from this terrible engine of rage and suffering, Gran rose up from his seat, drove to Fremont, deposited his mother and daughters at his sister's place, and headed to SFO to purchase a plane ticket to Egypt. He planned to pick up his son Akmal, who, he hoped, might keep him from killing Shakako while he attempted to save her life.

•
•

Shortly after being dropped off by an especially desperate taxi driver (most had not been willing to risk the journey from Kabul to Logar) near the market of Wagh Jan, Shakako walked past a local militia's checkpoint without much trouble at all because of her burqa and the confidence with which she ignored the militiamen's gaze. Dully hid underneath the furls of his mother's veil, clinging to her ankle as she walked through the markets, kicking up clouds of dust and runoff from the shops, passing butchers and carpenters and merchants, all of whom seemed to be wondering if the tall woman in the veil was not someone they knew or loved. Shakako and Dully made their way to the recently reconstructed bridge above the Logar River, marking the beginning of Naw'e Kaleh, just a few kilometers away from the home of Imam Qadir.

Shakako was elated. She stood on the edge of the bridge, her son at her side, taking huge gulps of the country air, that scent of wood smoke and grain, and her lungs hadn't felt this rejuvenated since the bygone days of her youth, when Soviet bombs had yet to scar her insides forever. Side by side, Shakako and Dully crossed the bridge into Naw'e

Kaleh and began to traverse trails and dirt roads, cutting through fields of grain and rows of chinar, and only occasionally crossing the path of another curious villager (in his pakol and dusmal and waskat and saplays and fake-gold-rimmed aviator sunglasses, Dully almost looked human). The trails and fields turned into corridors, into alleys, into makeshift mazes, surrounded on both sides by the high walls of interconnected clay compounds. Finally, after exiting one of these mazes, Dully and Shakako approached her father's old compound in Naw'e Kaleh, in front of which were the markers (two lonely flags held up by small piles of stone) indicating the exact spot where Fahim and Kadeem were ambushed by unknown gunmen nine and a half months ago.

In the wake of their mysterious murders, Shakako's family was forced to flee from their beloved compound in Logar and rent an overpriced apartment in Kabul. The motive behind the killings remained unknown because Fahim and Kadeem were so beloved in the village that none of the murderous militias, or the marines, or the Ts themselves, were willing to take credit for the ambush. Fahim had been a pharmacist who gave free inoculations to bedridden villagers. Kadeem was an engineer working on a communal well to be shared by the entire village. There was nothing ill to be said of either of them.

May Allah have mercy on their souls.

On the night Shakako found out about the murders, it was actually Dully who had picked up the phone and delivered the news, fumbling with the words "brothers" and "murdered" and "both of them" because his Pashto was not as strong as it needed to be that night. Gran rose up from his seat, the quickest he had moved in years, and held his wife to his aching chest, reiterating the logic of existence, "For to Him we belong and to Him we shall return," which did nothing at that moment to lessen Shakako's horror at the impossible news. "How did they die?" she kept asking all through the night, no matter how many times she heard that they were murdered. "But how?" she asked over and over, as in, "Through what terrible magic were the spirits in their bodies struck down by steel and fire?" As in, "How could it even be possible?"

Dully couldn't say. He had never known death like his parents, who, during the days of the Soviet war, had collected limbs and buried families, had heard children whimper for their lives before passing into silence, had known God's quickness and aim. In the days after the call, Dully was especially struck by the propulsive momentum of the news. It went from mouth to ear to phone, spread in hushed tones and prayers, told and retold, until every Afghan in

West Sacramento could recite, from heart, the exact circumstances of the murder of Shakako's beloved brothers, who had died yards away from their home, amid snowfall, innocently.

Kneeling before the markers of Fahim and Kadeem, Shakako whispered a dua and cried softly into the mesh of her burqa. Dully knelt beside her, lifting his hands as if he also meant to recite a prayer, but he said nothing to God or his uncles, all three of whom he had never really known and mourned only through his mother's grief. Somewhere distant in the valley, a bomb went off, and the tremors of the aftershock gently rocked the pebbles beneath Dully's feet. He felt exposed at that moment, at the mouth of the alley where his uncles had been ambushed, and out of a sudden, disorienting fear, Dully climbed into his mother's lap, navigated the shifting ripples of her burqa, and continued to pray. Shakako mistook Dully's fear for affection. She ran her fingers through the fur beneath his pakol and wondered, momentarily, if it would be so bad to fail in her mission to revert him. All her life, Shakako had known that her children, especially her boys, would grow apart from her, but the degree to which Dully had isolated himself in his studies still shocked her. The few times every semester she got a chance to see him, to chat or to listen, it seemed as if she were meeting a different Dully each time. Thinner, balder, weaker, sadder. More and more lonesome. More and more well read. Dully the Scholar, Dully the Philosopher, Dully the Historian. But the Dully in her lap, so small and vulnerable, reminded Shakako of the days when he was her student alone, when they would recite surahs and hadiths and the tales of Mullah Nasiruddin, when he knew no one else and nothing more and all the world was a mystery.

"We should keep going," Shakako said, but did not move.

Dully understood. He leapt away from his mother, scurried up the wall of his grandfather's compound, and, opening the gate from the inside, found that his mother needed no further prompting to enter her lost home. She led him through the orchard, past the apple trees and the empty cow pen, into the courtyard, where they inspected the abandoned bedrooms and the dying flower garden. Dully repressed an urge to frolic in the leaves. It had been years since Dully had seen his grandfather's compound, and he was alarmed by its degradation. He remembered how beloved he felt within its walls, with his mother's large, affectionate family, but now the compound seemed as desolate as his life at the university. A distant cousin had been hired as a groundskeeper, but he had neglected Baba's lilies and their rotting petals gave off such an intoxicating scent, Shakako became drowsy. Lying together in the courtyard's beranda, Shakako told Dully stories from when she first fled Logar in '82. At the time, she recalled, Fahim and Kadeem were so young, they thought Shakako was their second mother. Through mountain passes and battlefields, past borders and encampments, she had led her brothers away from the war.

Then she led Dully to the Imam's house.

"He's kidnapped," the Imam's third and most impudent wife, Gulalai, informed Shakako at the iron doors of her compound. She stood in the middle of the doorway, without inviting Shakako inside. "Just after Fajr," Gulalai continued, "he was snatched from in front of his mosque by a squadron of gunmen on horseback . . . Rahim's boys."

"Rahim is back in Logar?" Shakako asked, already tiring of the way Gulalai breathed, as if she were the only woman in Logar with ash in her lungs.

"He's been back for a few months . . . set up his own base in Shekha Kala . . . has his men running wild on horseback . . . carrying out raids . . . kidnapping imams. . . . If Qadir hadn't died so many times already, I would be losing my mind. . . ."

"Is he at the base often?"

"Hardly leaves . . . has a few boys in there to keep him company. . . . It's walking distance from here, you know, if you want to pay him a visit . . . maybe see if he hasn't killed my husband again. . . ."

"Maybe he'll offer me a cup of chai," Shakako said.

"I'm sure he'll offer you more than that."

"Look at this. The mouth. The balls. Where are your sisters?"

"Here," she said, and thrust the gate open to reveal two more women peering out from behind an interior wall. Imam Qadir's first and second wives quickly took cover, though it was clear Shakako had already seen them.

Without another word, Shakako walked off.

"It's the evil eye, my sister, nothing more!" Imam Qadir's second and most honest wife, Gulapa, shouted at the back of Shakako's head.

She pretended not to hear her.

———

●
○

By the bank of a thin canal hidden between a row of chi-nar trees and a tall field of corn, Shakako unfurled her hijab and was busy washing her face and arranging her hair when Dully asked her how she expected to convince a random warlord to free a political prisoner.

Fortunately, *this* warlord wasn't so random.

Before the war(s) had mutilated his soul and his body, be-fore he had adopted the moniker "Kung Fu," before he had been one of Shakako's many suitors, Rahim "Kung Fu" Ka-reem had been one of her enemies. What happened was that one morning Shakako's favorite cousin, Razia, went to fetch water from the Logar River when Rahim's elder brother, barely thirteen at the time, snatched Razia's dusmal, pro-nounced his intention to marry her, and sprinted away. With-out much thinking about it, Razia picked up a large stone from the bank of the river and hurled it in the general direc-tion of Rahim's brother, hitting him square in the head.

Rahim's brother collapsed and Razia fled.

Word soon spread that Rahim sought vengeance for his brother's injury, so Shakako directed an armed unit of her cousins to follow Razia from a short distance the next time she went to fetch water from the Logar River. Just as she had expected, Rahim attempted to launch a sneak attack, but before he could, Shakako and her girls fell upon him from the trees. Bloodied and bruised and thoroughly defeated, Rahim watched helplessly as Shakako climbed down from an apple tree, into his heart.

In the days and weeks that followed, Rahim gifted Shakako with one peace offering after another. Berries and candies and even a stolen baby lamb. Eventually, Shakako accepted a particularly smooth stone as a gesture of goodwill. They were friends for the one summer before they became too old to be seen together, which also happened to be the summer that Shakako's home was bombarded by an unceasing barrage of suitors. They came at all hours of the day, interrupting Shakako's life only to inspect her like a horse. "She's dark," the mothers of the suitors tended to say, "but her hips and her eyes more than make up for it."

Tiring of their visits, Shakako soon fell into a habit of brutalizing her many suitors with buckets of ice and cows' dung. Tales of her torment circulated the village, which only enticed more hardheaded men, including Rahim, whom Shakako denied with a bowl of shorwa and goat shit. But because Shakako had made such a weak effort to con-

ceal the pellets within his soup, Rahim held out hope for
his love.

Unfortunately, by the time the war got underway, the suitors started dying off and Baba felt he could no longer allow
his daughter to go unwed. He needed a warrior to look after
his family. Thus, a few months into the fighting, Shakako
was married to a mujahid named Gran. He was large and
dark bearded and ugly, but his ugliness (and his proficiency
with a shotgun) seemed to suit the atmosphere of the war.
Even on the day of their wedding, he arrived on horseback
with a machine gun hanging from his side and a bandolier
still strapped to his chest. Rahim, of course, didn't attend.

Having fled from his home in Logar, young Rahim was
said to have signed up with Hekmatyar's forces in the early
1980s, taking on the moniker "Kung Fu," and quickly earned
himself a reputation for treachery. When Hekmatyar's
Hezb-e-Islami started losing steam a few years later, he
switched from Hezb to Jamiat to Junbish to Ittehad in an
ongoing attempt to anticipate the final winner of a war
that would never actually end. Ultimately, he pledged loyalty to the US-backed government in Kabul, acquiring a
hefty allowance, a loyal squadron of battle-hardened militiamen, and, eventually, a brand-new base.

A few meters outside Rahim's base in Logar, Dully hid in the canopy of a mulberry tree, attempting to suppress a terrible urge to leap onto the rows of chinar trees planted along the bank of a bubbling stream. His tail chafed up against the rough fabric of his kameez, and his hairy toes were burning inside the cheap leather of his black saplays, but still he refused to strip down. He wished he had his phone. Fortunately, he carried a small notebook and pencil. To distract himself, Dully wrote: *The effect of these operations on Logar has been described by Borge Almqvist and Mike Barry, who visited the province in late summer and early fall 1982. The Swedish journalist Almqvist notes: "I entered into a country where every village has been bombed at least once since the war started. . . . Many villages are deserted, there are whole areas where the entire population run away to the camps in Pakistan out of fear of being killed in further air bombardments. These areas are so-called helicopter territories. When you move in them and you hear a helicopter you have 60 seconds to go. These areas have turned into the age before stone age. Civilization has gone back. This*

is before man entered Afghanistan in the very old times."
Barry's comments are even more sobering: "In our trip to
Logar province, . . . we crossed 12 villages including Dobandi,
8 of these villages, including Dobandi, were completely unin-
habited. One further village we saw destroyed virtually be-
fore our eyes. We were told that we should visit a village
called Altamor, and in the fog, we saw a great flash in the
distance. . . . And that evening and early the next morning
the first wounded came into where we were from Altamor,
telling us there is no more Altamor. . . ." Dully stopped and
recited, *There is no more Altamor,* in his head as if he were
reading it aloud, but could not recall the rest of the semi-
nal passage from Mohammed Hassan Kakar's *Afghanistan:*
The Soviet Invasion and the Afghan Response, 1979–1982,
which was a text Dully had read so many times, its pages
had been imprinted on his brain. *There is no more Altamor,*
Dully wrote again on the next page, but again his memory
failed him. He had lost the massacre . . . had annihilated
Altamor again . . . blessed Altamor . . . an entire village
wiped from the earth . . . wiped from Dully's memory,
which reminded him. . . . After climbing to the top of the
mulberry tree, Dully wrapped his tail around an outstretched branch, and leaning away from the breadth of the
leaves, he gazed out over the fields and the compounds and

the graves and the martyrdom markers strewn about the valley, and he searched the face of the Black Mountains for some sign of Hajji Hotak and his legendary shrine.

•
•

Having left Dully (and her burqa) in the branches of a nearby mulberry tree, Shakako visited Rahim's brand-new military base with the singular hope that her former suitor might still have in his heart some small measure of affection. Sitting in Rahim's office, which stank of hash and dried blood, Shakako explained to her former foe why she needed Imam Qadir, assuring Rahim that the old preacher was of no danger to him or anyone else. Rahim sported a thick black beard that ran all the way up his cheeks, and the hair beneath his cap flopped down onto his forehead so that almost all of his face remained hidden from Shakako. She searched his worn, battle-hardened skin for the little boy she once knew. Finally, he smiled—there was his smile—and asked Shakako if her old mujahid was still alive.

"Alhamdulillah, he is healthy," she lied.

"Has he gotten fat?"

"He's heavier."

"You've gotten fat too," he said.

"We've all become repulsive with age, haven't we?"

"I disagree. I think time has only made you more beautiful," Rahim said, and eyed Shakako like she was a wild horse or a new recruit.

Then he made her an offer.

"A kiss?" she asked loudly, into her chest.

"One kiss and you can have your imam."

"You'll give me a prisoner of war for a kiss?"

"Woman," he said, "if you come to my bed, I'll give you my whole fucking prison."

"Good," she said, and walked out of his office, having recorded the whole conversation on Dully's cell phone. Together, Shakako and Dully journeyed back to Kabul to swiftly report a case of military corruption.

The line to report incidents of government corruption stretched from the office on the second floor of the Fair Practices Department, out the courtyard, past six security checkpoints, and kept on going for two city blocks around the corner. Near the end of the line, a scrawny man waiting in front of Shakako—his face half-hidden by a black dusmal—asked Shakako about her little son, who obviously suffered from some sort of deformity, but before she could offer a lie, the man explained that he was waiting in line because his youngest and most beautiful son had been raped and murdered by an Afghan police chief. In one long burst, he recited his whole, sorrowful story. The child had been lured into the base with promise of work, but it had been a trap. "They used him for months, then tossed his body into a sewage canal near our home. He was as thin as a reed," the old man recalled. "He must have been so hungry." The woman in front of the man (wearing a dusty burqa) was also in line because her youngest son had been kidnapped, held as a sex slave, and subsequently murdered in a shoot-out with American troops. According to the mother, her son had been abducted under the direct order of Commandant Sarwar Jan because of how beautiful the boy had been. "Eyes like almonds," she said, "and lashes so long you could've swept leaves with them." Apparently, her son had been chained to a bed for months, until she managed to pay off a couple of underlings to free him. But by then it was too late. The boy couldn't live with himself. He signed up with the Ts and subsequently died attacking the same base where he had been held. After word of the debacle attracted some American journalists, a few stories were printed, the mother was interviewed, her son's grave was photographed, and Commandant Sarwar Jan was reassigned to a new base just outside Kabul. He never faced any real repercussions. In fact, almost all of the mothers and fathers in the line went on to explain to Shakako that they had already complained a thousand times over to government officials and news reporters and NGO activists about the rape and murder of their children, but because the commanders were protected by the US military, they would never be discharged or jailed or brought to justice. Now, every week or so, the parents waited in line only to meet with other parents whose sons had also been killed, so as to exchange photos and stories and garments of clothing, all the while commenting upon the terrible beauty that had doomed their boys. They hid their faces and refused to give their names. Some of the parents had come from as far as Kandahar and some resided within Kabul. They spoke Pashto and Farsi and they told their stories over and over to anyone who would hear them, not so much because they expected sympathy, or justice, but because their sorrows seemed so absurd when spoken aloud.

"We'll be heard," Shakako assured her son, though he

had said nothing to discourage her. "We're Americans and this city still belongs to America. We'll be heard."

•

Inside the second-floor office of the Fair Practices Department, the Kabuli bureaucrat sitting behind a two-inch-thick bulletproof glass booth peered up at Shakako as if he could see the angels frolicking from the single strand of hair jutting out of her otherwise hairless chin. She attempted to file a complaint written in Dully's academic English, only for the bureaucrat to ask if she had a permit for the monkey quietly sitting at the back of *his* office.

"That's not a monkey," she said, "that's my son."

The bureaucrat muttered something about another one going mad and called for the nearest guard. Dully, meanwhile, was on the brink of a breakthrough. He had realized that if he reoriented his dissertation project around the absence of any official record of the Hotaki massacre in Logar, the signs of its erasure would only strengthen his central argument regarding the discrepancies between the oral histories of Logari villagers and the official historical archives of the former British Empire and the modern nation-state

of Afghanistan. The project would then come full circle
through the oral accounts of the parents of the children
raped and murdered by government commanders. The spectacle of the line, of a system meant to perform accountabil-
ity and yet whose true purpose was to gather and conceal,
to collect and obfuscate, to allow the state to torture and
rape and murder perpetually, fit so perfectly into the devel-
opment of his argument (both thematically and historically!),
Dully began to consider which publishing press would be
the best fit for his groundbreaking book. *The violence of
erasure is perpetuated onto infinity in each instance of its de-
nial,* Dully typed and read and reread and momentarily felt
so proud of his clever sentence that he never saw the squadron of guards who had barged into the office to end his
academic dreams forever.

3

Poor Dully was stripped of his clothes and his phone and
all the other remnants of his former life. He lived in a sad
cage with forty other monkeys of varying breeds and sizes
and species, kidnapped from distant jungles and savannas.
All the animals in the Kabul Zoo—dirty wolves, diseased

ducks, scrawny horses, and a solitary bear—were visibly underfed and depressed, but the condition of the monkeys was especially appalling. Their cage was built upon a bed of dying grass and they had nothing to climb on because the bars were coated in a cheap plastic material that burned at the touch. They were hungry and sad, shedding fur and tears, and they attacked one another, often, for no reason at all. When Shakako had the chance to visit Dully, she slipped him a new phone through the bars of his cage, but because his fingers were bruised and burned, it took him a very long time to text.

Oo, he wrote, and nothing else.

He stood naked with the phone in his hands and did not attempt to cover his shame.

Shakako wanted to tear off her skin and cover him with it.

"I'll get you out," she swore on the name of Allah, the Most Merciful, the Most Just, and went on to relentlessly harass zookeepers and government officials, threatening lives and families and getting herself arrested twice. She visited distant family members, hers and Gran's, to see if anyone had any sort of connection that might get Dully out of the zoo. She even called up a few cousins connected to the Ts to see if they might arrange a bombing, but Shakako couldn't convince them of the strategic benefit of attacking an underfunded zoo.

When the zoo closed in the evenings, Shakako spent most of her nights at her father's apartment in Kart-e Naw, where her entire family (mother, father, two sisters, two widowed sisters-in-law, and six nephews and nieces) shared three bedrooms, each room containing its own shrine for Fahim and Kadeem. Shakako slept in the smallest room with her parents. Having lost his sons, Shakako's father, Baba, had taken it upon himself to complete all the daily outdoor errands. At seventy-five years old, he thought he could muster up the old strength of his youth, but his bones ached with every tremor in the city. Shakako's mother, Abo, hardly left her apartment at all and lived in a constant state of ill health, which she blamed upon the city itself. Every morning, Shakako told her parents a new lie about her plans for the day—land and loans and eligible brides—and every morning Shakako returned to the Kabul Zoo, smuggling herself in and out and assuming a number of different identities (visitor, relative, reporter, employee), until the keepers caught on to her tricks and hired extra female guards and plastered her visage on every cage and every wall, making it virtually impossible for Shakako to check on her imprisoned son.

•

Dully was withering.

The days weighed on him like months, and his body seemed to be aging at a rapid pace. His fur was falling out in clumps along his back and shoulders, his little belly had become bloated and tender, and even his eyelids felt too heavy to lift. He hardly slept at all. In the afternoons, when a keeper came by to toss buckets of fruit and insects and twigs through the bars of his cage, he could not bring himself to battle with the other monkeys for sustenance. Vicious baboons and powerful chimpanzees and even the smaller, wilder monkeys tore into one another for a tattered banana peel or a single cricket, while Dully remained in his corner of the cage—an unfortunate plot of real estate marked by its proximity to the makeshift latrine roasting all day long under the hot Kabuli sun—where he contemplated escape routes out of the cage or out of his body. Except for mealtimes, the other monkeys generally fell into depressive stupors, mindlessly roaming from one side of the cage to the other, almost zombified, but on occasion they could also burst into random fits of violence and savagely beat one another. It was the chaotic nature of these attacks that most unnerved Dully. Sometimes he could go days without being touched, living in a state of utter isolation, watching the zookeepers and the patrons and the other caged animals move about in patterns so routine, he felt he could predict their every single gesture—but then he might be beaten three times on the same day by three different apes. To stave off attacks, Dully chewed on the ends of twigs and scattered sticks, creating little spears and planting them in the dirt throughout the cage. More than anything else, these hidden weapons comforted Dully, and at night, when he slept upon the mounds in which they were buried, he dreamed of spears blossoming into trees, into orchards, into fortresses, into the beginnings of a nation that did not exist but could.

With time, Dully became so desperate to escape the corporeal realities of his monkey existence, he decided to pray. Five times a day, he made wudhu using the dirt in his cage and stood facing Mecca—as far away from the latrine as he could get—and performed salah. When the zookeepers took notice of Dully's miraculous habit, they created a new exhibit especially dedicated to his prayer and gave him his own rations of food, including vegetables and fresh fruit, which Dully promptly redistributed among his fellow monkeys. As a joke, the keepers provided Dully with a janamaz and tasbih, but were soon astonished to see him counting beads as if he were making dhikr. Before long, Dully felt himself torn between the performance of his prayers (and its commercial nature) and the sense of fulfillment these performances gave him. Years earlier, Dully had heard from his older brother, Akmal, that the Sufi practice of focused dhikr and chanting could lead to brief departures from the material realm, and although Dully had dismissed his brother's ideas at the time, he could no longer stomach the perpetual ache of his animal existence and attempted to purge himself of all attachments to the earth. Dully's dhikr, however, seemed only to root him deeper inside himself. He became more and more attuned to the internal workings of his own body. The beating of his heart. The squelching of his guts. The aching in his skin. The receptors at the ends of his fingers that sent messages up and down his arms, to the brain and back again, to tell him he was burning or bleeding or rotting or dying. His hearing heightened. His vision sharpened. His breathing calmed. His hands and feet no longer shook in the presence of the larger apes. The other monkeys took notice. They stopped attacking him, and, in fact, they even kept a respectful distance while he prayed.

In his state of perfect stillness, Dully began to see that he wasn't caged at all, that he was inside of a game, and that if he paid close enough attention, the rules for victory would be made apparent. To the zookeepers, Dully played the role of pious monkey well—praying all five of his prayers on time so that the keepers could announce the beginning of each salah beforehand—and he was rewarded with more food and trinkets and toys, and he continued to redistribute these spoils evenly among his monkey brethren, developing unspoken bonds of mutual benefit and respect, until he started communicating with his fellow captives through gestures and coos and shrieks and guttural noises he realized could be shaped into rudimentary, single-syllabic terms like "kha" and "wror" and "jang." He buried more weapons and dreamed of them blossoming. He prayed and profited and shared and listened and spoke and planned. He saw the one hundred flaws in the zoo's defenses. His captors were sloppy.

They could be outwitted.

They were only human.

About three weeks into Dully's imprisonment, Shakako received a call from an unknown number on her father's cell phone, and though her husband wouldn't speak when she answered, Shakako could tell it was Gran by the distinct huff of his nostrils' breath. He had just arrived at the Kabul International Airport with their eldest son, Akmal, his Egyptian wife, Fatima, and their two young children.

"Do you remember me?," Gran said after a few moments.

"I remember," Shakako said, though she had, in fact, forgotten, and went on to confess all her troubles to him in a mad jumble of sobs and stories, until Gran no longer had the heart to unleash the one thousand curses he had saved up in his neck and shoulders all throughout his arduous journey from Sacramento to San Francisco to Berlin to Cairo to Tanta to Dubai to Kabul.

At Baba's apartment, Gran quickly realized that his wife had been leveled by her recent ordeals. She had lost weight and color. Her billowing skirts no longer clung to her hips. Her hair looked thinner, and she smiled too much at nothing. His wife had become a wilted flower, and Gran couldn't have been happier by how angry this made him. Gallantly (he thought) he swore to her and God that Dully would be freed by the end of the day. And so, with Shakako and Akmal in tow, Gran left the apartment, rented a taxi, borrowed a cousin's handgun, and arrived at the Kabul Zoo just in time to find out that Dully had already escaped.

According to the zookeeper lying in the infirmary, half-dead but conscious, his arms and legs broken, a twelve-inch gash running from his armpit to his hip, forty beloved monkeys had banded together under the leadership of Dully, and in a mad operation involving a desecrated Quran, three separate suicidal diversions, and too many dead monkeys to count, Dully and his rebels fought their way out of the zoo and fled into the recently reconstructed sewer system beneath Kabul.

"If my son dies," Gran threatened the zookeeper, "you die with him."

"Inshallah," the zookeeper muttered, and passed out from the agony of his wounds.

•
•

In the coming weeks, TOLO played at all hours of the day and night in Baba's apartment. Shakako and Gran watched as televised news coverage of Dully's exploits quickly spread throughout the city. It started with reports that "sewer bandits" were robbing wealthy foreigners in the barricaded Green Zone of Wazir Akbar Khan. Eventually, the wrong diplomat got robbed and Vice President Abdul Rashid Dostum sent a couple of his goons into the sewers with bats and clubs. When the goons disappeared, Dostum dispatched a squadron of policemen with rifles and handguns. And when they also vanished, he resorted to armed units of the ANA with machine guns and armor. But no matter how many gunmen were sent down into the sewers, the expected echoes of gunfire never sounded. The soldiers simply disappeared.

No one seemed capable of hunting Dully down.

Not even his parents.

Gran and Shakako spent days shouting into manholes and tossing messages in bottles and pleading with their son during radio interviews, but the louder they called for Dully, the more resounding his silence seemed. At times, Shakako found herself blaming the internal structure of the city itself, and she ached for the days when Kabul's sewers were open and exposed, the city's muck as visible as its life, in the days before this secret, underground labyrinth had been constructed with billions of dollars, only for her son to go off and get lost in its corridors. She stopped using the indoor toilet in her father's apartment and would walk two city blocks to a local salon and shit in an outhouse because of how much she associated the sewers with her son.

As the weeks turned into months, Shakako became more and more offended that her rebel son had yet to contact her.

"He is technically an enemy of the state," Akmal attempted to console his mother after he caught her cursing into the kitchen sink. "He probably doesn't want to endanger us."

"He is also *technically* my son," Shakako responded. "It's not up to him whether or not I am endangered."

Shakako wasn't getting along with Akmal. Or his family. They all shared a single room in Baba's apartment, where it quickly became apparent to Shakako that Akmal had been wholly transformed into an Arab. His wife and children refused to speak Pashto or Farsi. He splayed his legs when he prayed. His English had taken on a slight Egyptian accent. He wore a white thobe in the house and seemed genuinely perplexed by the fact that his mother wasn't enamored with his stuck-up, stubborn wife, with whom Shakako still spent many hours watching TOLO news segments. In a televised press conference, President

Ashraf Ghani ordered a citywide lockdown after a series of protests had erupted because the families of the recently disappeared soldiers were demanding entrance into the sewers. Ghani had called upon US Special Forces to assist in the capture of Dully, but after an air force AC-130U gunship massacred an entire wedding party the week before, General John Nicholson Jr. was purportedly worried that attacking a pack of exotic monkeys in the sewers of Kabul might be looked upon unfavorably by animal rights activists in America.

"Cairo is just the same," Fatima told Shakako in English. "A madhouse."

Shakako did not disagree—but was certain that Fatima was wrong.

*

Over at their Zakia Ama's house in Fremont, Shirin and Shama had not heard word of their brother's exploits.

"Do as you wish," Zakia Ama had commanded as soon as they unpacked and settled in. So, they obeyed. Shama began cooking all sorts of delicacies, though her father had forbidden her from wasting time in the kitchen.

Her calculus homework lay unfinished in her backpack.
Shirin, meanwhile, was eating everything Shama cooked,
having abandoned her veggie smoothies under the direct
order of Zakia Ama.

"Fruit isn't food," her ama declared.

"But these are vegetables."

"Even worse!"

When Bibi attempted to order Shirin around (call your
mother, she said, complete your schoolwork, she said, perform your prayers, she said), her ama was always there to
deflect or distract, to whisk them away to Little Kabul, or
to host lavish dinner parties for her many friends. Widows
and divorcées, mostly, they strolled into Zakia Ama's house
wearing gaudy jewelry and designer handbags gifted to
them by the sons they had sent off on interpreter rotations,
back when an Afghan teenager from Fremont could make
an easy hundred grand in a single summer of teaching soldiers the cultural and linguistic complexities of a country
they had never visited. Shama served the snacks while Shirin poured the tea. She watched the cups of chai dwindle
to within a gulp of nothing and then rushed to fill them
up before the ladies noticed. The scent of baked cinnamon
wafted from the kitchen. Shama was experimenting.

Everyone stopped to sniff and sigh.

"My poor son," Bibi complained to Khala Kamara on the couch. "He's got no handle on that wife of his. I told him. So many times I told him to marry in the family, but in those days the fool couldn't see anything beyond the snout of his shotgun. Now look at him. Embarrassing us all."

"But why did she leave?" Kamara asked.

"I can't say. I know your mouth, Kamara. I won't say."

"Bad time to be in Kabul," Khala Mina jumped in. "My son has been in lockdown ever since the Taliban took the sewers."

"It isn't the Taliban," Bibi blurted.

"TOLO says it's a new insurgent group," Kamara said.

"Of course, they would say that. They don't want to admit that the Taliban are winning the war. The tide is turning, my son says."

"Your son says that?" Bibi asked.

"Yes, my son, the minister," Mina said.

"You know what my son says?" Kamara said.

"Now it's her son."

"What's wrong with my son?"

"The spy or the drug addict?"

"Aziz is not a spy," Kamara went on, "he is an inter-preter."

"What does your son say?" Mina asked.

"Aziz says it's monkeys."

"Monkeys!?" Bibi shouted because she could no longer contain herself. "Yes! Yes! Monkeys! And maybe the monkeys and the Taliban will join sides? For the sake of Allah, Kamara, do you hear yourself?"

•
•

The monkeys and the Ts ended up joining sides.

In the midst of the face-off between Dully and the government, the Ts took the opportunity to carry out several car bombings and machine-gun assaults on the outer edges of Kabul, killing over fifty policemen and twenty-something soldiers. The fighting was so prolonged and intense that militia forces, including a squadron led by Rahim "Kung Fu" Kareem, had to be called up from Logar. But just as soon as the militias arrived in Kabul, the assault abruptly ceased, and the Ts reemerged in Logar, easily conquering most of the interior villages in Mohammad Agha, including, of course, Naw'e Kaleh.

The very next day, the Afghan government promptly declared an unconditional military victory for having successfully purged the city of all insurgents.

"Does that mean Dully has been killed?" Shakako asked Gran and Baba and even Akmal, but no one could give her a clear answer until Dully himself had a chance to speak. He called from an anonymous number and spoke to Shakako in a terrible, grunting voice she could barely recognize.

"Mother," it said in Pashto, "how are you?"

"Abdullah," she replied, "*where* are you?"

"Where else?" he said, and invited his mother to Logar.

4

Dully no longer stood upright. Having renounced footwear forever, he wandered about the courtyard of Baba's compound on all fours like his monkey brethren, and although he still wore a smartly fitted kameez, he no longer attempted to hide his tail, which, in fact, he now used much like an extra limb. He ate with his right hand while sipping chai with his right foot, while giving orders on a burner with his left hand, while jotting notes with his left foot, while pointing a baboon in the direction of the tandoor khana with his tail. The rest of the monkeys lived in the orchard. They used the old cow pen as a barracks and passed their time swinging from the apple trees, collecting and evenly distributing the orchard's fruit, and waiting upon the call of Dully, whom they obeyed and loved with such a fanatic fervor, it made the local Ts a bit envious. Capable of tearing limbs and ripping flesh, prepared to charge headfirst into machine gunners, and utterly submissive to their commander, Dully's monkeys were the perfect soldiers, and he rewarded their loyalty by keeping them fed and warm and content and free.

Upon arriving at the compound, Shakako, Gran, Baba, and Akmal had been directed toward the beranda by a former government soldier turned insurgent, who politely offered them chai and kishmish. Dully appeared in the courtyard a few minutes later, conversing in whispers with a big bearded stranger who might have been a T. Purportedly, the local Ts had arranged a secret alliance with Dully in exchange for the use of his grandfather's compound and the support of his men. Baba was not pleased. "Offering me chai in my own home," he said, "as if I am *his* guest." Shakako hushed her father, fearing Dully might hear, but her son was so busy with his one hundred tasks at once, he couldn't perceive anything outside of an immediate five-foot radius. He sat before his family, ordering, chatting, eating, drinking, writing, noting, planning, and confirming military operations until he set those duties aside, paused for too long, and finally addressed his parents. He greeted them in a manner so formal, Shakako could hardly bear it. A part of her wanted to rise up and take Dully in her arms, to embrace him, or to choke him, but she felt uncertain before the strange men in the courtyard, before the primates rushing in and out of the orchard, and before Dully himself, who seemed, for the first time, wholly content with his primal self.

"Usually," Baba began, "a man asks permission before occupying another man's house."

"Well, it's good, then," Dully replied in his terrible, grunting voice, "that I'm no longer a man."

"The village won't stand for this long," Baba said. "My neighbors know—"

"Baba," Dully interrupted, "how far away from your house were your sons when they died?"

Baba said nothing for a few moments. He looked as if he couldn't recall the answer to Dully's question, as if it lingered somewhere on the outer edges of his memory. Eventually, mercifully, Shakako responded in his place. "It was just outside," she said. "You know that. They were ambushed in the alley."

Dully continued to address Baba. "But no one has any idea who killed them? None of your neighbors?" he asked.

Baba looked down at the chai he had been served but which he had refused to drink.

"It's a small village," Dully said.

"It is."

"But no one spoke."

"No one spoke," Baba confirmed.

"Abdullah," Shakako started to say.

"Is it possible?" Dully went on. "Is it possible that the whole village had gone blind and deaf for an evening? Let me ask you something else. If I could offer you their heads, the killers, would it be worth the price of this compound?"

Baba held his chai up to his face with both hands, as if to steady the cup. But he didn't drink. He seemed to be watching himself in the tea leaves. "You could find them?" he asked. "Truly?"

"When there is order, there will be justice," Dully said. "Do you understand? In the name of Allah, there will be justice."

Baba took a long sip from his cold chai and said that

he understood. Gran nodded in agreement, as did Akmal. But Shakako felt more perplexed than before, her questions having multiplied and intertwined and mutated, until the only thing she could think to say before Dully departed was, "Well, what about the Imam?"

Halfway out the beranda, Dully turned to his mother, and in a tone that was almost admonishing, he said: "The Imam will be free when Logar is free."

⠆

As word of Dully's insurrection spread across the World Wide Web, hackers and trolls and conspiracy theorists turned Dully's movement into an internet phenomenon. The campaign was called "Harambe's Revenge" and a series of memes propelled its popularity on Reddit, 4chan, 8chan, and Twitter. Dully's existence was debated on thousands of message boards by millions of anonymous users. His supporters referenced Afghan news reports and eyewitness testimony from soldiers and policemen who had purportedly seen Dully and his squadron in battle, but Dully's detractors simply brought up the fact that there was not a single shred of photographic evidence to verify his existence. That was, until an Afghan German correspondent from *Der Spiegel* visited Logar with a camera crew (and a security detail) for Dully's first-ever interview.

They set up in the orchard.

Framed by a backdrop of apple trees and dappled sunlight, Dully answered the correspondent's questions with a calm swagger unseen in an Afghan insurgent since the bygone days of Ahmad Shah Massoud. The interview went smoothly. Dully distanced himself from the Ts. He remained opaque about the exact political ideology his organization upheld. He referenced his past life as a scholar of history and violence. He lamented civilian murders and government corruption. He demanded the total withdrawal of foreign forces from Afghan soil. He advocated for the complete autonomy of the sovereign nation of Afghanistan. He used words like "the people," "injustice," "revolution," "exploitation," "raham," and "jihad." He even referenced Harambe's Revenge at one point. Clips of the interview went viral online. Some claimed that the video was a deepfake, that Dully didn't exist. Others said Dully's body was animatronic. A Hollywood setup. The conspiracy theories never died. Nonetheless, hackers from Russia and China began to fund Dully's military operations using bitcoin and the dark web. Cash flooded into Dully's online accounts from all over the world, and with this upsurge in international funding, Dully turned his grandfather's compound into a wartime fortress equipped with a weapons training camp and an exterior wall of steel. Dully's cousins and neighbors rushed to join his cause. The movement grew. Newly armed and reimbursed, his loyal warriors (both men and monkeys) were able to conquer larger swaths of Logar, all the way onto Rahim Kung Fu's base near Shekha Kala, until Rahim himself sent a message through intermediaries, offering to give up Imam Qadir for the safety of his militia.

Dully held a council.

By then, his advisers were made up of an incredible assortment of insurgents, mullahs, distant relatives, former policemen, former soldiers, current policemen pretending to be former policemen pretending to be rebels, apes, baboons, renounced Marxists, torturers, petty thieves, assassins, bandits, and boys barely over the age of seventeen. There also may have been a T or two in the mix, though no one could confirm such a claim. Advice was offered, hadiths were recited, surahs interpreted, the Imam's propensity for miracles was referenced, a hundred positions were argued over, but ultimately the decision came down to a single historical point: "Rahim never wins," a fifteen-year-old boy had said. "He only escapes to create more trouble."

The men all murmured in agreement and looked to Dully.

•
•

Unfortunately, Shakako did not find out about the decision to ambush Rahim until the next morning, when her husband nonchalantly mentioned it in bed. Shakako and Gran had been sharing their old wedding chamber for the past month, just two thin toshaks on the bare clay. The war or the countryside or his memories of the war and the countryside seemed to have awakened some old unbeaten artery in Gran's heart because he had become livelier than Shakako had seen him in years. He woke up at dawn and prayed with the fighters. He ate inordinate amounts of shorwa and rice but had lost his eternal gut. He spent most of his time counseling Dully and falling deeper into the machinations of the new war, which was only of course an extension of the old war, Gran's war, when he had been young and indestructible. Shakako witnessed all this from a distance. While Gran and Dully were busy with battle strategies and war council, Shakako found herself drifting out of the loop. Whatever information she gleaned, she picked up on the sly while cooking or washing or sweeping away flower petals in the courtyard. But, on occasion, she did manage to squeeze some intel out of her man.

"Rahim offered the Imam?" Shakako asked.

"Yes, yes," Gran said, "but we were able to convince Abdullah not to take him."

"But why not?" Shakako almost shouted.

"Your tone," Gran warned.

"Please explain to me why Dully didn't take the offer."

"Listen, I know that Rahim propositioned you. Everyone knows. And Dully understands—"

"No. Gran. You can't ambush Rahim."

"I didn't say anything about an—"

But before her husband could finish his lie, Shakako was already out of bed, donning her burqa, and off in search of her son.

Dully was *not* in the courtyard picking flowers with Baba, and he was *not* in the guest room learning Arabic from Akmal, and he was *not* in the armory examining his weapons, and he was *not* on the roof scoping for robots or God, and he was *not* in his bedroom in the highest corner of the compound reworking his maps of Logar, and he was *not* in the orchard training with the apes and baboons, and he was *not* in his makeshift library reading texts on guerrilla warfare by famous Marxist warriors, and he was *not* in the beranda discussing the minute delineations of Islamic law with the local mullahs—but Shakako did not falter. She went from one haunt to another, knowing Dully was never anywhere for too long because he tended to float about the compound as if he were searching for something indiscernible. He slept little and seemed very tired all the time. During important meetings and war councils, he would stare off into clay or lose his train of thought until someone advised him on a particular tactic or strategy, and he would nod yes or no because it hurt him to speak. More than at any other point in his life, even more than when he was being martyred by his studies, Dully had become so lonesome and solitary, so untouchable, that the air through which he walked stank of sadness.

Ultimately, she found him outside the compound, in a large potato patch, hidden within the foliage of an old mulberry tree. He lay prone upon a particularly long branch pointing toward the markers of Fahim and Kadeem, and he stared straight ahead, his black kameez covered in dust and splinters, occasionally jotting notes into his journal. Either because he was too focused on his task at hand or because he hoped to be rid of her, Dully did not acknowledge his mother's greeting.

Shakako, nonetheless, persisted.

"When Fahim was young," she told Dully, "he used to lie on that same branch and hunt for moles. He spent entire nights up there. Protecting our potatoes."

"It's almost ironic, then," Dully said, more to himself than to his mother, "that this was the same branch from which he was shot."

For a moment, Shakako wondered if Dully had lost a certain capacity for understanding the violence of his remarks or if he purposefully meant to hurt her. Either way, Shakako stripped off her burqa, hiked her skirt up to her knees, and began to climb the limbs of Fahim's mulberry tree, until she made it all the way to Dully's branch. Then she swung her legs over onto one side, leaned against the tree trunk, and inhaled deep, rasping breaths of the country air. To her left, the fields and the orchards seemed to roll away from the valley before halting at the edges of the Black Mountains. To her right, Shakako watched the markers with Dully, and the alleyway beyond the markers, and she realized that her son was right. This was the spot. The assassins would have been able to see her brothers coming from a distance . . . within firing range. It was perfect.

"Remember," Dully said, "it was snowing that night. Most likely, the assassins wouldn't have been able to see their faces, just the headlights of their vehicle."

"How many of them were there?"

"At least two. One to keep lookout, and another to aim. Besides, it was freezing."

"They kept each other warm, then."

"They might have been huddled together, the assassins, just moments before the hit."

"Then what?"

"They would have waited for the headlights to fall forth from the alley, and then the shooter would have fired from this very tree branch, before fleeing into the fields below."

"Are you certain?"

Dully turned and nodded but was no longer sure.

"Fahim and Kadeem were shot from close range," Shakako said. "Your assassins might have waited in this tree, they might have huddled on this very tree branch, but they went up close for the final act."

Dully closed his notebook and sat up and faced his mother.

"Abdullah," Shakako said, "how many ambushes have you arranged? Ten? Maybe twenty? And how many of those ambushes were against foot soldiers? Boys, really."

"What boys?"

"The plan doesn't make sense."

"Rahim won't see it coming *because* it doesn't make sense."

"Who told you that?"

"No one . . . ," Dully started to say but stopped. It wasn't true. That very phrase "*because* it doesn't make sense" had been uttered by one of his many advisers. He couldn't even say with certainty which one. And it wasn't that he doubted his men's loyalty or, really, his own authority, but lately he had been overwhelmed by the feeling that the more he commanded and controlled, the more he needed to be advised and convinced and the less control he had over anything. He had, in fact, heard of the boys his men had killed near the bridge above the Logar River. Six vengeful teenagers—with only two rifles and a few knives split up among them—had stumbled right into one of Dully's patrols. His men weren't ordered to massacre the boys, and yet they weren't punished either. The boys were blotted from the earth; their families were offered substantial blood payments, and word of the massacre barely left the village. There weren't even any new markers set out. Dully considered building some sort of a monument for the dead boys. He considered writing about their deaths. He spent many moments waiting to be moved, to be haunted, but as the battles and ambushes continued, the specters seemed only to accumulate, their curses or pleas turning into a chorus, into a gentle droning, like rain patter or white noise. There was just so much more to do, so many more to kill or absolve, beginning, of course, with Rahim.

"I know Rahim," Shakako said. "I defeated him once before, and I can defeat him again. But this plan. It's not the way."

"Then what do you advise?" Dully said.

•
•

But listen—

Before the reports of the massacre trickled in, before their weapons were loaded and polished and kissed and blessed, before Gran reconvinced Dully to doom them all in the solitude of three in the morning, before she almost managed to save her son, Shakako had already known that Rahim, her old foe and ally, would have anticipated any ambush with an earlier ambush of his own. And so it happened that Rahim "Kung Fu" Kareem fell upon Dully and his men near the Logar River in much the same way that Shakako had ambushed him almost three decades earlier.

Akmal died instantly, torn apart by a hurricane of bullets in a state of transcendent devotion to Allah. The tasbih he carried fell to the earth unharmed. Gran was shot nine times through his neck and shoulders and died painlessly at the foot of a mulberry tree. Minutes earlier, he had walked the roads of his village, shotgun in hand, feeling as he had felt in the glorious days of his jihad, when martyrdom beckoned to him from every mountain pass and lightning bolts propelled his every movement. Dully was shot seven times in his torso, nearly dying on the road before two apes managed to carry him back home just in time for Shakako to hold him, once more, on the edge of the orchard in her father's compound.

In his mother's arms, Dully touched his skin and his wounds, mystified by the fact of his bleeding, no longer certain if he retained the form of a monkey or a man, or if it even mattered, and he reached up to touch his mother's face, but noticing the angels that swung from the single strand of hair still stubbornly jutting out of her otherwise hairless chin, he stopped and understood. Patches of Dully's fur were clumped together with dried blood or clay, and Shakako picked at this clay or blood, carefully, so as not to tear his fur, but her son still pulsed feverishly with pain. Then, underneath an apple tree, in the dappled shade of the breathing leaves, Dully cooed a quiet prayer his mother could not hear, before shitting seven small pellets in her lap and dying with his mouth open.

Cradling her son's body, Shakako picked at the dried clay or blood, just as gentle as before, as if not to hurt him, and she dropped these flakes into a pile near her legs. She carried on like this for hours—all throughout the early morning—holding out hope that her son's corpse might be reverted to its human form, but Dully stayed as he was: a small monkey, shot to bits, tattered and lonely and so monstrously fragile, Shakako would not allow anyone else to touch him.

That was, until she was interrupted by an (un)expected guest.

Alive, again, Imam Qadir stood at the entrance of Shakako's home, with the corpse of her husband on one shoulder and her eldest son on the other.

The bodies were laid to rest in the orchard.

Wrapped in beautiful silken linens of green and gold, the corpses of Gran and Akmal resembled large cocoons from a distance, whereas Dully's body, small as it was, looked more like an infant swaddled in cloth, forgotten in the forest of some child's fairy tale. The distinct scent of lilacs wafted from their martyred bodies, and because there was no fear of decay, Shakako had asked Baba to retrieve her mother and her sisters and her aunts and her cousins and her daughters and her daughter-in-law, without whom, she said, the janaza would not be carried out. In the meantime, Imam Qadir sat with Shakako in the orchard, just yards away from the corpses, and he attempted to comfort her with stories of martyrdom and mercy, of miracles and dreams, until he landed upon a tale that caught her attention.

"When the English began their massacres on the outskirts of Naw'e Kaleh," the Imam recalled, "Hajji Hotak was the last of our villagers to flee into the Black Mountains, wherein he was promptly captured and executed by an English regiment. This is true. But the part of the story that everyone forgets is that Hajji Hotak was only captured because of his mother. At one hundred and ten years old, Hajji Hotak's mother, Bibi Hotak, had begged her son to leave her at home and to flee with the rest of the village at dawn. Surely, she argued, the English would not harm a woman as old as her. But Hajji Hotak did not believe in the mercy of Englishmen. Certain that the invaders would cut down his mother in her bed, he strapped the old woman to his back and staggered off toward the Black Mountains. Well, as it's told, shortly afterward the English marauders caught up to Hajji Hotak. They separated him from his mother, stood him up at the mouth of a cave, and prepared to execute him by firing squad. Bibi Hotak knelt just a few yards away. She heard seven rifles fire and watched seven pellets strike her son square in the chest, before he fell with a resounding thud and died with his mouth open. The Englishmen left Bibi to die in the mountains, but as soon as they disappeared, she recited a quick prayer for her son and began to gather small stones and even pebbles to bury Hotak above the earth. With time, day after day, week after week, year after year after year, Bibi Hotak built the entirety of the shrine of Hajji Hotak, which stands to this day, but—and here's my point—although everyone remembers the death of Hajji, no one ever recalls the miracle of Bibi's mourning."

At the end of his story, the Imam gazed at Shakako with such a look of tenderness and undying love, it enraged her.

"Get out," she told him.

"What?" the Imam asked, not knowing that his eyes had betrayed his story.

"Go to your wives, you fool," she said, and tossed the Imam out of her home, along with the soldiers and the monkeys, who all fled into the Black Mountains to be hunted down, one at a time, by government forces under the command of Rahim "Kung Fu" Kareem, and because none of the men in her family could stay in one place for too long, for fear of the killer robots that lived in the sky, Shakako's compound of mourning was filled to the brim with ladies, including her young daughters, Shirin and Shama, who had landed in Kabul, hours earlier, with Bibi. In the haze (or the clarity) of her mourning, Shakako completely ignored her mother-in-law and apologized to her mystified daughters.

"I've lost all your gold," Shakako told them, weeping. "Please forgive me."

The girls obliged her.

On the foot of the steps into the beranda, where Bibi had gathered all the older ladies to whisper duas and recite the Quran, Shirin held Shakako against her pudgy belly (still rich with baby's fat) and sang songs about Jannat she had learned in Sunday school, while Shama sat in the warmth of the tandoor khana, baking flatbread of the fluffiest textures to absorb her mother's tears and to fill her empty stomach, which was where they all once lived, or so it was said, before God gave them form.

The Haunting of
Hajji Hotak

You don't know why, exactly, you've been assigned to this particular family, in this particular home, in West Sacramento, California. It's not your job to wonder why. Nonetheless, after a few days, you begin to speculate that the suspect at the heart of your assignment is the father, code-named Hajji, even though you have no reason to believe that he has ever actually completed the hajj pilgrimage to Mecca. In fact, Hajji hardly leaves home at all. He spends hours at a time wandering around his house or his yard, searching for things to repair—rotted planks of wood, missing shingles, burned-out bulbs, broken mowers, shattered windows, unhinged doors—until his old injuries act up, and he is forced to lie down wherever he is working, and if he happens to be in the attic or the basement, or in some other secluded area of the house, away from his wife and his mother and his four children, sometimes he will allow himself to quietly mutter verses from the Quran, invocations to Allah, until his ache seems to ebb and he returns to work.

When Hajji has exhausted himself, he often retires to the living room, where he watches murder mysteries or foreign coverage of conflicts in Islamic countries. If his wife, code-named Habibi, is in the kitchen, and if she isn't already chatting with one of her many friends, most of whom you know Hajji despises, he will request a cup of tea and ask about his mother's health, which is never very good, but Hajji's wife doesn't tell him this, because his mother, code-named Bibi, is sitting just a few feet away, and though she doesn't acknowledge her son's presence, Bibi is always listening.

From early dawn, when she wakes to pray, until late at night, before she falls into a fitful sleep, Bibi nests in a corner of the living room, on the farthest edge of the second couch, and listens to the television at an incredibly low volume, listens to her son and his wife in the kitchen, to her grandchildren on their phones, to the Quran on an old radio that she smuggled out of Afghanistan forty years ago, to the flushing of the toilets in the house, to the wind in the trees that her son planted near her window, to the gentle burbling of her oxygen tank, and to the constant thrumming of the house, and she reports back all that she hears to her only living brother, in Afghanistan. Thanks to Bibi's keen ear for even the most minute details, her calls are thorough and uncompromising. She knows when her grandchildren are constipated. She knows when her son and his wife are secretly fighting. She knows who is peeing too loudly or cheating on exams or missing prayers. Through Bibi's many reports to her brother, you begin to gather snippets of Hajji's history: his former life as a mujahid in Afghanistan; his trek from Logar to Peshawar to Karachi to California; his wedding; the births of each of his children; the children's gradual loss of Pashto; their gradual increase in insolence; the trucking accident that destroyed the nerves in Hajji's neck and shoulders; the court cases that led to nothing; the betrayal he felt when his second-eldest son, code-named Karl, decided to become a Marxist while studying at Berkeley; his depression; his total disillusionment with the American justice system; his anger; his rage; his softly bubbling fury.

In another life, you think, Bibi might have been a spy.

Hajji's eldest son, Mo, gets home from his job at Zafar's butcher shop in the evening. He wears a blood-splattered smock, an Arabic thobe, and a heavy beard. Every night, Mo's mother scolds him for not having washed his smock, which smells like a massacre, and every night Hajji defends his son, who smells, he says, like a man. Mo begs his mother's forgiveness with a laugh and sits beside his father. In English, Mo asks Hajji about the current condition of the ummah, which translates roughly to "community" but actually refers to a supranational collective of Islamic peoples.

"They hope to destroy our ummah," you record Hajji saying, in English, before he gives a recap of all the bombings, massacres, war crimes, protests, shootings, kidnappings, and assassinations that have occurred in the past twenty-four hours. Mo listens quietly, only occasionally asking a question or muttering a vengeful prayer.

The rest of Hajji's children arrive as dinner begins.

Lily, the youngest, sneaks into the kitchen and asks her mother which dishes have been prepared without meat.

Lily has recently, and secretly, become a vegetarian. Two weeks earlier, she came home weeping to her mother after having witnessed the vehicular maiming of a duck that was crossing the street with a line of her ducklings. Lily had cradled the duck in her death throes, surrounded by her little ducklings—which, Lily swore, were crying out for their mother. Together, Habibi and Lily wept for the little orphaned ducklings. Later that day, Lily informed her mother that she could not bring herself to eat the chicken korma she had prepared, and Habibi decided not to scold her (a decision she would come to regret). At first, it was only chicken, but then Lily confessed to her mother that she could no longer stomach beef or lamb, the rest of the culinary trinity of Hajji's household. Habibi made an effort to explain to her daughter that vegetarianism was a slippery slope toward feminism, Marxism, communism, atheism, hedonism, and, eventually, cannibalism. "Animals are animals," her mother explained deftly, "and humans are humans, and when you begin mixing up the two you will find yourself kissing chickens and eating children."

Lily swore that it was a matter not of ethics but of physical repulsion, and that with time, inshallah, she would be able to eat all her favorite dishes again. Habibi relented, and for a few days the secret remained solely between mother and daughter, until Mary, Hajji's elder daughter, turned toward her sister one afternoon, in the room they had shared since Lily's infancy, and asked her how much weight she had lost.

"None," she said too quickly, laughing. "I'm as chunky as ever."

But she *had* lost weight. Two pounds.

"Then why do you look so pale and self-righteous?" Mary asked, continuing her interrogation. Sharp, uncompromising, and with an excellent eye for weakness—a trait that, you assume, she inherited from her grandmother—Mary has many talents (deception, introspection, manipulation, a high pain threshold, and embroidering) that are wasted in Hajji's household, where the girls are allowed to go only to school or to the mosque and then must come straight home.

It's really a tragedy, you think. She could have been a fine spy.

In the end, Lily confessed her sin to Mary, who immediately mocked her. "Idiot," she said. "You're short enough as it is. How do you expect to get taller without protein?"

"I'll eat beans."

"Beans? How many beans? This room isn't ventilated enough for you to be eating beans all day."

"Please," Lily said. "Don't tell."

Mary laughed and promised to snitch as soon as she could, which was a lie, of course, because Mary wasn't the sort.

During dinner, Lily is always careful to serve herself a heaping portion of chicken or kebab or kofta, but while she

eats her rice and fried vegetables, Mary, an avowed carni-
vore, nonchalantly clears away Lily's meat. Hajji, fortunately,
never notices. He eats with perfect focus. In total silence.
And with his fingers.

Habibi, on the other hand, hardly eats. She is all questions and stories. She wants to know about Mo's butchering,
Mary's studying, Lily's friends, and even Marvin's gaming.
In response, the children tease her, which often upsets Hajji,
but Habibi always takes it in stride. She is—in your professional estimation—the beating heart of the household. Not
only does she take on most of the chores, she also actively
organizes the entire social life of the family—dinners and
parties and showers and gatherings and even the occasional
communal prayer. Seemingly at war with the hundred silences that fill her small house, she is almost always on the
brink of shouting in Pashto or Farsi or English or sometimes Urdu. She chats so much on the phone, outside in the
yard, inside in the kitchen, with her gloomy husband, her
spiteful mother-in-law, her eclectic children, and her many,
many friends that you end up spending half your time at the
office skimming through hours and hours of Habibi's gossip, translated from your audio recordings by an officially
sanctioned team of Afghan American interpreters, who are
only ever provided with fragments of her statements, in the

hope that they won't figure out whom, exactly, they are in-
terpreting. Habibi's relentless chatter, however, is not completely useless. Every night before bed, she calls her family
in Afghanistan, some of whom still live in a small village in
Logar Province, which, according to your research, is currently under the control of the Taliban.

The word comes up sometimes amid Habibi's barrage
of Pashto and Farsi. Her "baleh"s and "bachem"s and
"cheeka"s and "keer"s.

"Taliban," she will whisper into her phone, as if she
knows you are listening.

Just the sound of it makes your heart race.

After dinner, Marvin and the girls rush off to their
rooms while Mo, his parents, and Bibi drink tea in the living room. Inevitably, the conversation turns to Mo's pros-
pects for marriage. Habibi has a niece in Kabul, a midwife
and a beauty, who speaks English, Pashto, Farsi, and Urdu.
"She is almost too good for you," Habibi says, laughing.
Hajji has a niece in Logar, only sixteen, wholesome, holy.
She has memorized half the Quran, and her father is a respected mullah in the village. What Mo's parents don't know
is that Mo is already in love with a girl at Sac State. They are
constantly messaging, conversing, and Snapchatting. Mo

writes her secret love poems on his laptop. Horrendous verses that he is rightfully embarrassed by. Sometimes, when he thinks he's alone, he recites his poems quietly.

His love, you hope, will save him.

At night, Hajji and his wife are the first to go to bed. The next morning, they will wake up at dawn—Hajji because of his pain and Habibi because of Hajji's pain. Both Marvin and Mo pretend to fall asleep, but when Mo thinks Marvin has passed out he sneaks downstairs with his laptop, and as soon as he does, Marvin climbs out of his own bed, performs wudhu, and begins to make up all the prayers he missed throughout the day. Though Marvin has earned a 3.8 GPA in his first semester at UC Davis, though he works part-time and donates money to Afghanistan, his parents often scold him for not praying, not reading the Quran, and Marvin never utters a word in self-defense. And yet here he is, in the middle of the night, praying in secrecy, away from the approving eyes of his mother and father and brother and grandmother, reciting verse after verse from the Quran, in a voice so soft and melodic that it almost brings tears to your eyes.

Downstairs, Mo descends into forums. Swaddled in his father's woolen shawl—the very same shawl that Hajji used to wear in the days of his long-ago jihad—Mo watches clips of American bombs falling on Iraqi cities, Afghans bearing witness to ISAF executions, Muslim boys being burned alive in Gujarat. He watches these clips for hours, his head bobbing, his eyes bleary, until his beloved, mercifully, notices that he is online and commands him to go to sleep. Upstairs, Mary is reading Mo's messages. She has hacked into his Facebook account and watches his conversation play out in real time. She is a ghost on his profile, always careful to read only what he has already read and to leave everything else untouched. Such potential, you think, such a pity. Lily, in the bed next to Mary, is sketching pictures of ducks and ducklings and ponds and ducks crying into ponds and ponds expanding into oceans and ducks in flight and ducks walking and ducks dying, and she takes pictures of these charcoal portraits and posts them to a private Instagram account, which Mary can also, secretly, access. In the room adjacent to the girls, Hajji and his wife have a quiet argument about his wife's brothers. You recognize their names and suspect it has something to do with the fact that they were employed as interpreters for the US military in Afghanistan. Hajji, you know, considers these men to be traitors. Eventually, Habibi turns away from her husband, mutters something under her breath, and cries herself softly to sleep. Hajji does nothing to comfort her. He sits up in bed, wheezing with pain or regret, and stares out the window at the dark street, where Mo is now shadow-boxing beneath a streetlight. Tucked away in her corner of the house, Bibi sits up at the same moment, in the same manner, and stares out her window at the same streetlight. She, too, watches Mo strike at invisible enemies.

When the family finally sleeps, you listen to them dream.

In the course of the next few weeks, you search for clues, signs, evidence of evil intentions. But to no avail. Life merely goes on.

Hajji repairs a window he broke while attempting to repaint his mother's room.

Cold floods the house.

Bibi moves into the boys' room, and the boys sleep in the living room. No longer able to sneak away from each other, they carry out long conversations before falling asleep. They discuss their family's finances, their suspicion that their father is hiding bills from them. They plan to confront him but never go through with it.

When they sleep, both of the boys snore, Marvin whistling and Mo sort of growling, and the girls, whose bedroom is closest to the living room, complain to each other all night. The timing of the boys' snoring is uncanny. There is a certain rhythm to it. When Mo murmurs, Marvin bursts, and when Marvin quiets, Mo roars. The girls refer to it as "the symphony." Eventually, though, the girls fall asleep and you become the sole listener.

Mo notices blood in his stool but doesn't go to a doctor.

Mary earns a 4.3 GPA for the semester, and Hajji buys doughnuts for the whole family. They all sit in the living room eating doughnuts and drinking tea, and Bibi jokes that now they won't have to sell Mary for a pair of goats. The whole family laughs as though in a scene in a sitcom.

While her husband is out buying supplies from a hardware store, Habibi receives a call from her parents, in Kabul, and discovers that her mother is seriously ill. She tells no one and leaves to visit her brothers across town. Soon afterward, Hajji returns home to find her missing. He goes from room to room, calling her name. For the first time in weeks, Bibi speaks to her son, informing him that his mother-in-law is sick.

Tech workers from the Bay Area have moved into the neighborhood. Property taxes are rising. Bills stack up. Hajji needs help but won't tell his sons, because he doesn't want them to take on more work. He borrows money and credit. He buries the bills at night like corpses.

Habibi receives another call from her parents. There will be an operation. It's the heart, of all things. Habibi tells only Hajji, but Bibi, of course, finds out.

In a moment of weakness, Lily eats a Slim Jim that she shoplifted from a gas station near her school. At home, she vomits the processed meat for several minutes. Though everyone assures Hajji that Lily will be fine, Hajji insists on taking her to the emergency room. "As long as we have Medi-Cal, why take the risk?" he argues. An hour later, Hajji and Lily return home from the hospital, and Hajji informs his wife that Lily has become a vegetarian. He asks her to keep it a secret. "For now," Hajji says, "she doesn't want anyone else to know." Habibi promises not to tell a soul.

One afternoon, while her father sleeps and her mother cooks, Mary shuffles through Hajji's mail and discovers past-due bills, three or four from the same creditor. She picks a few of the most urgent (electricity and internet) and rushes upstairs. On Poshmark.com, she sells her own lightly used sweaters and jeans and T-shirts, which she has embroidered with characters from popular animes—Sailor Moon and Totoro and Naruto—and, in the course of a week, pays her father's bills online.

Habibi tells Marvin about his grandmother's upcoming surgery. "Do you think she will forgive me for abandoning her in that city?" she asks him. Marvin pretends to pause his video game, even though he is playing online, in real time. He sets his controller aside and listens to his mother's fears without responding. He is killed over and over again.

The stack of bills lightens, but Hajji hardly notices.

When her husband is out, Habibi calls Karl in Berkeley. They chat about his stomach, his rent, his studies, his protests, and his prayers until Habibi begs him, once again, to renounce communism and come home. Karl argues that his father, more than anyone else, should be sympathetic to his cause. Habibi begins to weep and Karl mutters an excuse and hangs up. You wonder which of your colleagues is surveilling Karl.

While Hajji watches Al Jazeera—video footage of a young Afghan farmer being executed by an Australian soldier plays on the screen—Mary curls up next to him and picks at the flakes of dried skin in his beard as she did when she was four years old. According to Habibi, this was her special ritual before sleep. Now Mary has a bottle of olive oil in hand, a tiny dollop of which she pours into her palm and runs through her father's beard. The execution is played again. After being mauled by a dog, the farmer, Dad Mohammad, lies on his back in the middle of a field. His knees are drawn up to his chest, and he is clutching red prayer beads. A soldier stands over him with a rifle. "You want me to drop this cunt?" he asks. There is the sound of a shot, and the footage cuts to black. When Mary is gone and the news segment is finished, Hajji sits alone in the living room with the TV turned off. He runs his fingers through the moistened strands of his beard and seems surprised by its softness.

On the night before Habibi's mother's surgery, one of Habibi's brothers visits for the first time in months. Mary is the only one who doesn't acknowledge him. In their shared room, Lily attempts to persuade her sister to forgive their uncle for his many insults, attacks, jokes, attacks disguised as jokes, and threats. But Mary refuses. "Mom will understand," Mary says, but you're not so sure. That night, Habibi and her brother sleep on a red toshak in the living room and quietly pray for their sick mother. In the morning, the news is good, and you cannot help sighing with relief.

Six months into your assignment, you begin to doubt

your purpose. Hajji is falling apart. His doctor has advised him to undergo spinal surgery that may leave him paralyzed. In another era, in a different body, perhaps Hajji could have been dangerous. But here, now, debilitated by pain, the old man is no threat at all.

You should update your superiors. You should advise them to abort the operation. But you won't. Not now. Not when Mary is about to apply to colleges, not when Mo is planning to propose, not when Marvin is making new friends on campus, not when Habibi's parents are applying for a visa to the States, not when Hajji is deciding whether he will go through with the surgery, not when Bibi is losing touch with her brother, not when Lily is on the brink of an artistic breakthrough. There's too much left to learn.

But then, on a cold summer night, when the rest of the family has driven down to an aunt's house in Fremont, Hajji heads up to the attic to fix a pipe. You watch him prepare his tools and climb his ladder and enter his soaking attic, and in a fine mist of leaking water, Hajji fidgets with the pipe until he mutters, "Shit," in Pashto. He crawls back through the water, but on his way down he slips off the highest rung of the ladder and falls onto the hard tile beneath him. Though the fall must have been only ten feet or so, Hajji has landed awkwardly and broken his leg. He lies on the floor, on his back, staring up at the attic from which he fell. You know for a fact that Hajji has broken this leg once before, during the Soviet occupation, when a Kalashnikov round pierced his fibula and forced him off the battlefield for six months, during the heaviest period of fighting in Logar, and that this injury probably saved his life, and that his living—while his brother died, while his sister died, while his cousins and friends and neighbors all died—has haunted him his whole life.

A minute passes. Two. You know that Hajji always forgets his cell phone in the kitchen and that the kitchen is approximately twenty yards away from the spot where he lies on the floor, unmoving, and that he will have no other choice but to drag himself there and call for help. And yet he doesn't move. You listen for his breath and hear him rasping. Water drips from the trapdoor to the attic, and Hajji lifts his hands and washes his face and his arms and his hair as if he were performing his ablutions. It's at this point that both you and Hajji notice the small puddle of blood forming under his head.

Hajji pleads to God, and you hear him, and you answer.

The ambulance arrives shortly afterward.

The next day, as soon as he returns home from the hospital, Hajji purchases a phone recorder on Amazon and, when it arrives, has Marvin hook it up to the landline. No one questions him. No one argues. He listens to hours and hours of recordings in his bedroom, alone or with Habibi, and during awkward moments of silence, pauses in conversations, he stops and rewinds and listens again. "Do you hear it?" he whispers to Habibi in Pashto. "The breathing?"

She waits and listens again and nods her head.

You know this is impossible. You know there is no way for them to hear you, and yet, when you are listening to a conversation and there is a pause, a silence, you find yourself holding your breath.

Hajji becomes relentless.

He searches for you on the phone, in the streets, in unmarked white vans, in the faces of policemen, detectives in street clothes, military personnel, and his own neighbors. He searches for you at the hospital, at the bank, on his computer, his sons' laptops, in webcams, phone cameras, and on the television. He searches for you in the curtains and in the drawers of the kitchen and in the trees in his backyard, in the electrical sockets, in the locks of the door handles, and in the filaments of the light bulbs. And, even as his family protests, Hajji searches for you in shattered glass, in broken tile, in the strips of his wallpaper, the splinters of his doors, his tattered flesh, his warped nerves, and in his own beating heart, where, through it all, the voice whispering that he is loved is yours.

ACKNOWLEDGMENTS

Thank you to my teachers: Doug Rice, Yiyun Li, Hellen Lee, David Toise, and Lan Samantha Chang. Thank you to Lucy Corin, Pam Houston, Justin Torres, Alexia Arthurs, Margot Livesey, Jess Walters, Mat Johnson, and Elizabeth Tallent for your early notes on these stories. Thank you to Karan Mahajan for your thoughts, advice, and support throughout these last few years. Thank you to Amy Goldman for persuading me to take my first creative writing class in high school. Thank you to the Truman Capote Literary Trust, the Iowa Writers' Workshop, the UC Davis Creative Writing Program, and the Wallace Stegner Fellowship for providing me with time and space to write. Thank you to Jin Auh, my agent, and Laura Tisdel, my editor. Thank you to both teams at Wylie and Viking. Thank you to Brigid Hughes, Megan Cummins, and the entire staff at A Public Space for publishing my first short story when I was just a starving grad student. Thank you to Deborah Treisman, Adam Ross, Sarah Thankam Mathews, and Michael Ray for editing and publishing my stories. Thank you to Jesmyn Ward for selecting my work for *The Best American Short Stories 2021*. Thank you to Tanzeen Doha for your unceasing support. Thank you to Sandra Cisneros for your comments and words of advice. Thank you to Fatima Kola, Pam Zhang, Brandon Taylor, Bassam Tariq, Rajbir Singh, and Muneeza Rizvi for being early readers and commentators. Thank you to my sisters, Rana and Breshna, for providing vital feedback. Thank you to my brothers, Jalil and Marwand, for being my most honest critics. None of these stories are completed until they receive your seal of approval. Thank you to my wife, Nazifa, for your love and support. Your stories bring new light to my life. Thank you to my Athai for her tales. Thank you to my Mor and Agha, you've stood with me from the beginning.

Ultimately, all praise be to Allah (subḥānahu wa-ta'ālā).